BINGO UNDER THE CRUCIFIX

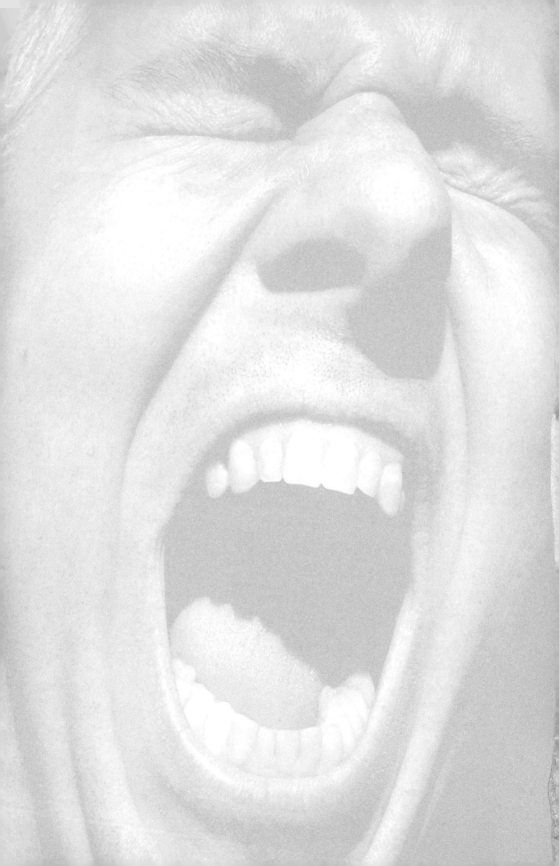

BINGO
UNDER THE CRUCIFIX

A novel by Laurie Foos

COFFEE HOUSE PRESS

2002

A PAPERBACK ORIGINAL

COFFEE HOUSE PRESS is an independent nonprofit literary publisher supported in part by a grant provided by the Minnesota State Arts Board, through an appropriation by the Minnesota State Legislature, and in part by a grant from the National Endowment for the Arts. Support has also been provided by Athwin Foundation; Beim Foundation; the Bush Foundation; Buuck Family Foundation; Elmer L. & Eleanor J. Andersen Foundation; Lerner Family Foundation; McKnight Foundation; Patrick and Aimee Butler Family Foundation; The St. Paul Companies Foundation, Inc.; the law firm of Schwegman, Lundberg, Woessner & Kluth, P.A.; Star Tribune Foundation; Target, Marshall Field's, and Mervyn's with support from the Target Foundation; James R. Thorpe; Wells Fargo Foundation Minnesota; West Group; Archie & Bertha Walker Foundation; Woessner-Freeman Family Foundation; and many individual donors. To you and our many readers across the country, we send our thanks for your continuing support.

COFFEE HOUSE PRESS books are available to the trade through our primary distributor, Consortium Book Sales & Distribution, 1045 Westgate Drive, Saint Paul, MN 55114. For personal orders, catalogs, or other information, write to: Coffee House Press, 27 North Fourth Street, Suite 400, Minneapolis, MN 55401.

Good books are brewing at coffeehousepress.org

LIBRARY OF CONGRESS CATALOGING-IN-PUBLICATION DATA

Foos, Laurie
   Bingo under the crucifix : a novel / by Laurie Foos.
      p. cm.
   ISBN 1-56689-133-7 (pbk. : alk. paper)
   1. Dollmakers—Fiction. 2. Brothers and sisters—Fiction. 3. Infantilism—Fiction.
   1. Title

PS3556.0564 B56 2002
813'.54—DC21   2002071281

FIRST EDITION
1   3   5   7   9   10   8   6   4   2

PRINTED IN CANADA

Acknowledgments

For their abiding friendship and attentive readings, I thank my friends
Ellen Cooney, Carol Magun, Susan Segal, and Judith Taylor.

For allowing me a glimpse into both her studio and her rare and particular
genius, I thank renowned dollmaker Lisa Lichtenfels.

For courage and inspiration, I thank my dear friend Cody Collett.

For his editorial guidance and for being a great champion of my work,
I thank Allan Kornblum, my editor and publisher.

For time and solitude, I thank the MacDowell Colony.

And for being all things loyal, loving, and true, I thank you, Michael.

For Michael,
and in memory of my beloved grandfather,
Dietrich Foos

Which is easier,
to say, 'Your sins are forgiven you'
or to say 'Rise and walk'?

(LUKE 5:23)

PROLOGUE

She wasn't expecting the baby that day. Ever since her period had stopped and she had sneaked into the bathroom at home to watch the faint purple line slide across the white box of her pregnancy test, she'd never really thought of herself as "having a baby." Once or twice she had used the word "pregnant," whispering it to her reflection in the mirror, but she had never put herself and the word "baby" in the same sentence. Instead she began to imagine him as a being named "Bubba," and sometimes at night, she envisioned him as large and fish-like with eyes blinking in the cloudy fluid of her womb. At times he provided comfort for her alone in the darkness of her bedroom, but she had been vigilant about not thinking of him as remotely belonging to her. He was a castaway that had gotten trapped in her mid-section and could not get out.

She'd told no one about him. One day, a girl from Biology class asked her what she was hiding under the heavy jackets and sweatshirts, and even then she hadn't answered. She was sure, though, that her brother Josh knew. She didn't know how, exactly, but when she'd started sneaking into Josh's room at night to take some of the old sweatshirts he kept on the floor of his closet, he hadn't told their parents. When she'd left the house that morning after eating breakfast and trying to hide the queasiness she'd so often felt, she saw the way Josh had looked at her, as if he'd seen right through her, through the thick padding of material that hid her bulging stomach, as if he'd seen the fetus inside her free-floating in the womb.

Josh had smiled when she'd gathered up her backpack to leave for the day and said, "Good luck today, Darlene," leaning on the word "luck," as if he weren't wishing for her to become queen at the homecoming parade, but for something much bigger. It was the same smile he wore when he looked at the books and videotapes he kept in his room, the ones their mother had forbidden him to show to Darlene again after she'd vomited that first time in the kitchen sink and blamed it on the pictures Josh had shown her.

At first the pain was little more than a tightening of her stomach muscles, the kind she felt when she did crunches or when she'd held her legs in the air for so long that night when it had happened. The wait had seemed interminable as she lay there, and she'd imagined herself with her crown in a white dress, waving, until he'd finally collapsed on her, and she'd simply rolled away. In the bathroom later that night, she'd scrubbed away the remnants of him with a soapy washcloth and told herself she'd wiped away any damage that might have been done.

As she made her way into the girls' locker room, most of the others were too busy to see her take the bunch of towels from the linen closet and slide her duffel bag into the stall. Everyone was buzzing about who would be named homecoming queen that day, and she'd heard rumors that she was the favorite. She felt a sudden flurry of excitement at this news and wished she could close her eyes and have Bubba removed like the abscess that had once infected her wisdom teeth. The pain spread through her groin as she sat on the cold porcelain while the band played in the distance.

The others scurried out of the locker room at once, giggling in groups as they headed out to the football field, and then she was alone.

Luckily, it didn't take long. She'd prayed for that many nights, and she silently thanked God for listening, even though she wasn't sure she believed in him at all. If there were a God, she thought, he would be somewhat like Bubba, amorphous and buoyant. Carefully, she arranged the towels on the floor in a kind of nest to catch the blood and the fish-like thing she'd called Bubba. The one part she'd remembered about the films they'd shown in Biology class was that there would be a lot of blood. She wished she'd studied harder.

With both hands around the sides of the head, she pulled him out, never sure what was so slippery in her hands, whether it was the head or shoulders or the squirminess of the torso. When her hands could not hold on any longer, she opened her fingers and let go.

She glanced down and saw him, then closed her eyes again. A boy. Bubba. She'd been right.

No cries rang out, no muffled sounds, only the quiet of the locker room and the frantic scrape of her towel sopping up the blood on her thighs and ankles, knots of blood that ran down her legs and soaked through the towels in enormous red blossoms.

She sat dazed for several minutes when she heard someone calling her name.

"Darlene! Darlene! Are you in here?"

She stood up and plunged both hands into the toilet then flushed repeatedly.

"Darlene Mulholland! Where are you?"

With her hands swishing in the bloody toilet water, she managed to speak.

"I'm here," she said. "I'm in here."

Suddenly it seemed everyone was calling her name. Cheers erupted from the field outside.

"Hurry!" someone squealed. "Come on! You're our queen!"

She stood up on the tile floor and felt the blood rush to her head, steadied herself with both hands on either sides of the stall.

"I'm coming," she said. "Just a minute, I'm coming."

She unzipped the duffel bag and removed the white tulle dress, the one she'd bought weeks ago with her mother. White had been a mistake, she thought, but then she remembered what the saleswoman had said when she'd seen Darlene alone in the dressing room with her rounded belly. Tulle was best. Tulle could hide anything.

"Thank God for tulle," she breathed, as she pulled the dress on and zipped it up the back.

She slipped her shoes on, which were white to match and had bloody scuff marks on the bottom, though thankfully the dress was so long, no one would see. Then she slid open the lock to the stall door, stepped over the pad of bloody white towels, and closed the door behind her.

When Chloe got the call that her brother Irv had become an infant, she was only surprised by the fact that he hadn't become Spider-Man. For years Chloe had been waiting for the call telling her that Irv had finally succeeded, that after all of the years of comic books and costumes, web designs and spider infatuation, he'd finally managed to turn himself into his beloved superhero. He'd wanted to be Spidey ever since she could remember, but a baby was another matter entirely. This, she realized, was a stunt she'd never expected, not even from Irv.

"Your brother Irv's gone and become a baby," her mother said evenly, as if she'd been rehearsing before placing the call. "I found him on the front stoop with a note stapled to his blanket. I nearly tripped right over him."

Chloe was struck not so much by the news that her brother had transformed himself, but by the fact that her mother referred to him as "Irv," the nickname Chloe had given him in childhood for reasons she could no longer remember. Her mother had always hated the nickname and had forbidden Chloe to use it in her presence. Irv was such an ugly name—a name for a lecherous old man, her mother had always said—which was exactly what Chloe had intended.

She took a long drag on her cigarette and blew the smoke out slowly, watching the puffs drift across the table and hang suspended over the halogen lamp in the corner of the room. She tried to think of something unexpected to say, something quick and surprising that would take her mother off guard, like her mother's use of the name Irv.

"Become a baby," she repeated. "My brother Irv has become a baby."

Her mother coughed loudly into the phone, thick rasps that rang through the receiver.

"Yes, your brother," her mother said, louder this time, her voice rising as if she were speaking to someone hard of hearing. "Your brother Ralph," she said, using his proper name now, "is now an infant. A newborn, straight out of the womb. And Ruth is gone. She took off and left him behind with nothing but a note."

Chloe said nothing for a long time. She held the cigarette between her fingers and watched as the smoke wrapped around itself and floated over the newspaper she'd been reading. People had been wondering what went on inside Irv's head for years, she thought, though she had tried her best not to be one of them. He was a big baby, his wife, Ruth, forever complained whenever she had a moment alone with Chloe. All he ever wanted was his mother. Ruth was eight months pregnant, and Irv had reached the age of thirty-six without ever having learned to operate a washing machine or cut his meat with a serrated knife, preferring instead to lift a piece of steak with his hands and suck the flesh off the bone. He still had all of the Spider-Man figures from his childhood and had only stopped sleeping on superhero sheets when he'd gotten married. He managed a comic book store full of teenage boys with whiteheads and mothers who washed their damp sheets.

"How do you know it's him?" Chloe asked, thinking for a moment that some reckless teenager might have panicked after giving birth and left the baby on her mother's steps after loosing the infant in a movie theater restroom. These kinds of things happened all the time in the New York papers. In the past several months there had been a rash of what reporters called "drive-by births" on Long Island. Months earlier, a fifteen-year-old had been tried as an adult and been sentenced to fifteen years after delivering a baby girl behind a supermarket and leaving her beside an ATM machine in the shopping center. Just last week the homecoming queen at a nearby high school in an affluent Long Island suburb had delivered a ten-pound baby boy during halftime. She then took her triumphant ride across the football field in a convertible with roses in her hand, waving as the janitors sifted through bloody towels in the girls' locker room. Chloe had just finished reading the latest article about the homecoming queen and had wondered what had made her run.

She'd have liked to have spoken to these girls, to ask them how they had managed to hide their pregnancies even from their parents, and more importantly, from themselves. Both girls had said repeatedly that they'd never considered what they'd delivered as "real babies." Just years before they'd been playing with baby dolls. Maybe they'd thought these infants had been dolls, too, which was a concept that Chloe, as a dollmaker, could readily understand.

"Oh, it's Ralph, all right," her mother snorted. "A mother never forgets."

Slowly Chloe picked up the newspaper and stared at the photograph of the homecoming queen taken from her jail cell. Her thin prison uniform sagged on one side, revealing a creamy shoulder. Chloe wondered why they hadn't been able to find a uniform to fit the young girl properly. The girl's lips seemed to tighten in pain, and she looked very cold.

"Okay," Chloe said finally, stubbing out her cigarette, "what do you want me to do?"

Her mother took a deep breath and let it out in a rush.

"You've got to come," her mother said. "I can't do this alone. Your father won't even look at him, and Aunt Chickie gets in her own way. I don't even know who to call."

When Chloe didn't answer, her mother cleared her throat.

"Please, Chloe," she said. "He's your brother, for God's sake."

Chloe considered telling her mother that God had nothing to do with Irv's being her brother; she was sure of that. She thought of poor Ruth with her swollen belly, lugging her infant husband back home to Mother and then running off. Now she would be forced to give birth on her own, without Irv there to hold her hand, wipe the sweat from her brow, or perform whatever small gesture he might have been able to manage. Wherever she'd gone, Ruth had not only a baby on the way but a baby/husband to worry about. Even the homecoming queen, alone in a jail cell with her crown in tatters, seemed better off by comparison.

"I'll be there," Chloe said finally, standing up to hang the receiver on its cradle. "Wait for us to come. Nathan will know what to do."

Without waiting for her mother to answer, Chloe hung up the phone and held it down on the cradle, hard, then lifted it off the hook to make sure the dial tone had returned. She set the receiver on the table and waited for the buzzing to begin, proof that no one could get through. Slowly she shuffled down the hall to her bedroom, an unlit cigarette perched between her fingers.

Nathan sat up when he saw her. Bunches of index cards crunched beneath him as he moved to a sitting position.

"What's the matter?" he asked, stopping to cross out a line he'd written with the Cross pen Chloe had given him for his birthday several years before. He was not averse to using a good felt tip if necessary, but said the right pen afforded his words an authority that no other pen had come close to.

She sat beside him on the bed, her shoulders hunched.

"Irv's become a baby again," she sighed.

She was suddenly shocked at the calmness with which she'd taken all of this in, her mother's voice on the phone, her brother's body shrunk back to infancy. In some strange way, she realized she'd been waiting for this to happen, that he'd always had a much better chance of returning to babyhood than he'd ever had at becoming Spider-Man, no matter how hard he'd tried.

Nathan was a professional party planner, though his real love lay in writing scripts and directing. But party planning involved orchestration of the best kind—stage directions, blocking, even set designs with the added bonus of celebration. Once he'd thrown an elaborate shower for a celebrity at a posh hotel and had the chef bake a cake in the shape of a fetus with long strips of banana licorice for the umbilical cord. He'd written a monologue for the fetus which a child actor in a bonnet and matching booties delivered to the expectant mother. At a Bat Mitzvah, he hired a singer to dress as a rabbi and serenade the young girl with "It Had to Be You." For his and Chloe's wedding, he'd composed congratulatory lines for every guest on the receiving line.

"People never really know what to say at family functions," he'd said when Chloe initially balked at the idea. "Why not give them a little help?"

And in fact, the guests had appeared one by one with index cards at the ready to deliver their lines. Some had even taken bows. Her family had come to rely on Nathan's penchant for scripts at holidays, always asking that he write the specs for Easter and Christmas dinners.

"I never know how the hell to say grace, even after all those years in Catholic school," her father had once said. "At least now I can always count on Nathan to give me a good line."

Nathan shuffled through his index cards as if searching for a phrase appropriate to the situation, though Chloe knew he wouldn't find one.

"Maybe it's not him," Nathan said, dropping the index cards on the bed. "Maybe it's some abandoned kid like the one that homecoming queen just dumped. Maybe it's not Irv at all."

"No," Chloe said, "it's Irv, all right. My mother's sure it's Irv. And I promised her we'd come."

Nathan reached for a fresh packet of index cards.

"We'd better get started," he said. "We'll need to know what to say."

As she sat smoking, Nathan listed all the questions Chloe wanted to ask:

1. Had Irv shrunk down to newborn size, his gums pink with new life, the hair on his body vanished, leaving his skin smooth and smelling faintly of baby lotion?

2. Was he conscious of his newfound infancy, crying out to his mother like the shrunken man in *The Fly*, trapped in the web forever, his little man's head squeaking for help?

3. Were images from the womb still swirling through his mind, his eyes glazed over with film, the whole world a gauzy collage of faded colors and newness, his adult life shucked away like dead skin?

4. How had he managed it? Had he (a) willed himself back or (b) had it come upon him like a dream, his mind swimming while his chromosomes did a crazy dance, scrambling themselves into a gurgling mass of diaper rash and drool?

Nathan passed each of the index cards to Chloe and waited for her approval.

"There's a problem with the second question," she said, leaning back on the bed. "He'd certainly like the web associated with *The Fly*, but he'd be a spider for sure. A real bloodsucker."

Nathan made a notation on the index card and pressed the end of the pen to his chin.

"That's a good point," he said. "But I'm sure that will go right over their heads."

While he continued scribbling lines on his index cards, Chloe tried to imagine if Irv were capable of doing something quite so willful, leaving Ruth with a nursery filled with stuffed animals meant for a real baby, not a thirty-six-year-old man masquerading as an infant. Poor Ruth, Chloe thought, as she took deep drags on her cigarette. No wonder she'd run. Ruth was nine years older than Irv and had certainly babied him, but Chloe was sure that even Ruth hadn't banked on a husband who would sneak back to infancy just when she was ready to deliver.

If nothing else, Chloe told Nathan, she was sure that being a big baby was not endearing to Ruth—or to any of them, for that matter. Even her mother had sounded horrified.

"Horrified," Nathan wrote in block letters before getting up from the bed. "Good word. We may have to use that one."

As Nathan moved about the room packing their bags, Chloe took the newspaper and cigarettes into her work room where the latest in her "Bingo Lady" doll series lay half-stuffed. The doll's saggy breasts still needed to be sewn and padded; her limbs hung loosely from her polyfill-stuffed body. The Bingo Lady dolls had become extremely popular in the last year after she'd debuted the exhibit—*Waiting to Wait*—at an annual doll show. Four needle sculpted women huddled together at a wooden table, looking expectantly at one woman's card with just two numbers left for the jackpot. Since then, she'd been bombarded by requests from collectors and gallery owners. Her friend, Gloria Rollins, a dollmaking guru, was planning to set up an exhibit on game-playing later that year. Gloria had once weighed nearly three hundred pounds but had gotten herself down to the one-fifty range, though she still wore muu-muus that hung about her shoulders like deflated tents.

"It's important not to forget who you've been," Gloria was fond of saying. "Every dollmaker has a history."

In the doll world Chloe was known as Esther Bing, a name Nathan had come up with one night while planning the couple's entrance at a silver anniversary party with a Humphrey Bogart theme. All the guests had worn trench coats and smoked cigarettes which was what had inspired the idea of Esther Bing as a chain smoker. She liked the idea of hovering over her dolls with a cigarette pressed between her lips in her Esther Bing persona. The smoking had quickly infiltrated her normal life as Chloe, since she spent so much time working on the dolls. Still, even with the smoking, no one in her family had ever guessed that she made dolls for a living. No one knew it was Chloe who had created the Bingo Ladies.

As Esther Bing, she got herself a P.O. box and a social security card and ordered cartons of cigarettes through the mail. Esther Bing provided a kind of anonymity that being Chloe Taft had never afforded her. When they'd married, she'd decided to retain her maiden name and not take on Nathan's, which was "Whittenstone," a name too long for perfecting the signature she'd come to depend on after being asked so frequently by doll collectors to offer her autograph. Her mother had been displeased by Chloe's decision not to take Nathan's name.

"You'll get so used to being Chloe Whittenstone that you'll soon forget who Chloe Taft ever was," her mother had admonished, though

Chloe thought that forgetting who she'd been was not something she aspired to do.

Since her father, the Big E, had achieved a certain degree of notoriety in the World's Strongest Man contests, Chloe had developed an uneasy relationship with fame, blushing even when Nathan's name appeared on the backs of invitations. As much as she loved dollmaking, she still hated the exposure that went along with attending conventions and doll shows. She felt much safer going as Esther Bing.

She always gave her dolls a history, and sometimes Nathan even wrote lines that he thought the Bingo Ladies might say. "Come on, O 75," or "This caller's time has come and gone." This particular doll had been a frequent jackpot winner who carried around a handful of twenty-dollar bills, which Chloe had cut from parchment paper and dyed green. Her name was Marilyn, and she'd had a run of bad luck recently, which was reflected in her tightlipped smile and the deep lines that Chloe had needle-sculpted under her eyes.

As she held the doll in her hands, she added wisps of ash-stained cotton that she used for touches of gray in the Bingo Lady's red mohair. Nylon doll skins and bits of fabric lay spread across her work table. Now that Irv had become an infant, Chloe sensed that this might be the last doll she'd be able to finish for quite some time. The smell of lint permeated the air, and the Bingo Lady's face seemed to twist in pain, as if the doll could sense the dread Chloe felt in the pit of her stomach.

Perhaps this doll was right, Chloe thought, as she sat among the pieces of cloth and thread that lay strewn over her work table. Perhaps Marilyn's luck had run out.

As if to prove this very point, she spent the rest of the evening sewing bits of red nylon to the doll's thighs, bumps of flesh that rose up her skin like a series of spider bites.

Homecoming Queen Leaps to Own Defense

Associated Press

Greenleaf Point, NY

In her first interview since the recovery of bloody towels from the locker room at Sagamore High in the upscale town of Long Island's Greenleaf Point, homecoming queen Darlene Mulholland told reporters, from her 6 x 9 jail cell, that she remembers little of the day she abandoned her infant boy.

"I did have a baby, that much I remember," she said. "And I tucked him into some fresh white towels where he'd be safe, you know? I would have come back for him. But then I heard them all cheering my name and the band playing. I ran straight out to the field before I could tell anyone. I mean, if you miss your chance you lose to the runner-up. I did what any girl would do."

Students at Sagamore High recall an aggressive campaigning that lasted for weeks. Mulholland and runners-up often wore sashes to school; some had even designed crowns for extra credit in Home Economics.

When asked why he thought Mulholland had left the baby, Sagamore

Sharks running back Steven Baker said, "She wanted to win. Homecoming can be cutthroat."

Mulholland is expected to appear before a grand jury where it is believed she will be indicted for endangering the life of a minor and first degree abandonment. When asked how she intends to plead, Mulholland voiced her opinion despite the objections of her attorney.

"It's not my fault that I won," she said. "So I'm not guilty. One hundred percent not guilty."

While Nathan packed the car, Chloe sat replaying the conversation with her mother in her mind. This had been one of the few linear conversations she and her mother had ever had, she realized. She had asked a question; her mother had given a direct reply. Talking with her mother had always been a messy business, as her mother so often broke off into long patterns of weak associations. She was never sure if her mother was really listening. Interesting dialogue, Nathan said, was not without its segues or harmless digressions, but her mother's mode of speaking could not be easily categorized.

"I don't know if it's that she's completely tuned out," he said, "or that the noise of whatever's going on in her head is just too loud for other people's words to get in."

Sometimes Chloe became so frustrated by talks with her mother that she paced from room to room, smoking until the curves of her ears turned red. At Nathan's insistence, she would recount the dialogue for him, complete with pauses and the nasal lilt of her mother's voice. He transcribed the conversations for further study and left them on Chloe's work table. No matter how much she pored over them, though, she'd never been able to understand them any better.

As she turned this conversation over in her mind once more, Chloe wondered what they were going to do about Irv. Why was it that her mother always assumed she'd have all the answers? How could she, of all people, know how to take care of Irv when avoiding him was all she'd ever wanted to do? It was something she wasn't proud of, thinking of her own brother in that way, but sometimes late at night she imagined his hands poised above her, the pale fingers curving, short black hairs scattered across the knuckles growing long and twisting down around his wrists. The hands floated, disembodied above the bed, and in those moments she felt her mind momentarily split from her body. She had to open her eyes whenever this feeling came, touch the alarm clock, let one foot fall on the floor, or pinch at the flesh in the crook of her knees to remind herself she was alive.

She wondered what the hands would look like now that they'd regressed to infancy. It was funny, she thought, taking a drag on her cigarette, that she hadn't thought to ask her mother how Irv now looked as a baby. In the black-and-white photos of her mother's albums, Irv's eyes were large and always open, his head snug in crocheted hats tied in loopy bows under his chin. He wrapped his mouth around his fist, his lips curving upward in the corners. In all the photos of Irv as an infant, Chloe had always felt her mother's presence lurking near the edges where the photograph ended, waving in her cotton dress, her mouth puffed up with pride. Even when she couldn't be seen, Chloe knew their mother stood waiting with pacifier in hand, like a mouthful of love.

Chloe stubbed out the cigarette and got up from the table when she heard Nathan calling that they were ready. She was about to lock up the house when she caught a glimpse of the newspaper on the floor. A photo of Darlene Mulholland, the homecoming queen, appeared on the front page. She sat forlornly on a cot in her cell, her hair shorn at the sides. At the parade Darlene had been photographed in her crown with long spiral curls hanging down below her shoulders, waving in her white gloves from a convertible. When the photo first appeared, bystanders at the game had remarked at how flushed and bright her cheeks were, but after learning what she'd done, they'd said she looked "peaked and guilty, just as she deserved to look." Now the curls were gone, her hair shaved almost to the skull on both sides, knotted strands still hanging down her back. Beneath the photo, the caption read, Homecoming Queen says aliens stole her baby. Shaves head in protest.

Chloe snipped the article with a pair of kitchen scissors and tucked it into the pocket of her jeans. The homecoming queen's baby had been gone nearly a week, and since the news broke it had been all people could talk about. What would possess a young girl to leave her bouncing baby boy wrapped up in towels while she stuffed wads of cotton between her legs, to run out to the cheering crowd with a crown on her head? Most people thought the homecoming queen deserved whatever was coming to her, but Chloe felt a deep sympathy for the young girl. Something about the look on her face told her that the homecoming queen had already suffered enough.

It took nearly three hours to make the forty-mile drive to her parents' house. Normally Chloe would have insisted on driving because of Nathan's fondness for tailgating semis and passing on the right, flashing his high beams at old ladies in Buicks with their gnarled hands gripping the wheel as they did thirty in a fifty-mile zone. Although gentle in so many ways, Nathan possessed a wild streak that came out whenever he slipped into the driver's seat. He refused to wait behind the lines of cars that dogged him wherever he traveled on Long Island.

With this news about Irv, though, Chloe simply couldn't muster up the courage to face a wall of traffic, drivers who refused to signal, a series of short on-ramps with little room to merge. She imagined horns blaring as she pressed the gas to the floor and struggled to make her way up to highway speed before being rear-ended by a sixteen-year-old with a brand new Trans Am and a license he'd gotten last week. She'd become so accustomed to Long Island that she no longer gave people the finger or blew out her breath when traffic suddenly stopped after cruising speeds of sixty-five miles per hour. Living close to New York had its price, she'd told Nathan after a brief stint upstate, where he'd been reduced to games of Pin the Tail on the Donkey at house parties for three-year-olds. She knew how helpless the traffic could make you feel when there was nothing ahead but miles of cars, the smell of exhaust seeping through the vents. Life on Long Island, she said, was one long desperate attempt to get a short distance away from where you'd been, only to find you'd hardly moved at all.

When she handed Nathan the keys, he passed her a packet of index cards bundled in rubber bands.

"I'll give you all the best lines," he promised. "That's one thing you can count on."

Before they set off Chloe rolled down her window and lit her first cigarette of the trip. She blew thick clouds of smoke out the window and sifted through the index cards. All of her lines had been written in blue ink, while the others had been underlined in red. Some of her possible responses included:

FORGET ABOUT IRV. I CERTAINLY WOULD.

MAYBE WE SHOULD ALL JUST LEAVE HIM ALONE. WHO REALLY WANTS HIM BACK?

NOT ME, NOT ME.

And then finally:

WHO KNOWS WHAT IRV DID?

BINGO!

Nathan, of course, knew what bingo had meant in her life, but none of the others would understand. She threw her cigarette out the window as they headed onto the entrance ramp of the Long Island Expressway and held the index cards so tightly that her fingers cramped.

The traffic stopped suddenly at the exit for Greenleaf Point. Reporters climbed onto the hoods of cars with binoculars poised. A large white van with the name of a local news station stenciled on its doors was overturned at the exit ramp, wheels spinning, the cameraman screaming and shaking his fists.

"It's that homecoming queen," Nathan said, craning his neck out the open window. A group of police officers hurried to the exit ramp and began directing traffic, waving their white-gloved hands in the air and blowing whistles. With her eyes closed Chloe tried to imagine herself at her work table with a brush in hand, ready to fill in the latest Bingo Lady's features with colored pencils. Coral for her cheeks and lips, soft black for her eyelashes. Suddenly, as Nathan jerked the wheel and sped around the overturned van, the index cards fell from Chloe's hands and spilled onto the floor in front of her. When she tried to gather them up, several of the cards blew out the window and floated in the air behind them.

"Shit, shit," she breathed, rolling up the window and scrambling to gather up the others from the floor in front of her. She banged her head on the dashboard, the pain bringing tears to her eyes.

"Don't worry, babe," Nathan said, taking one hand off the wheel and laying it on her knee. "There are lots more where those came from."

Chloe glared at him, shifted in her seat, and leaned her head against the window, pressing a hand to the space where her forehead throbbed. She watched the news van and the lines of traffic become smaller and smaller in the distance. Normally she would have begged him to slow down, but she was too preoccupied with the business of rearranging the cards to think about anything else. At least with the cards in her hands, she could think of other things besides Irv.

When she'd finished shuffling the cards, she reached inside the pocket of her jeans where she'd pressed the photo of the homecoming queen. She smoothed the creases in the homecoming queen's face, her fingers sliding over the corners of the photo where the long curls had been. She wrapped the cards in the newspaper clipping and pressed them against her chest to keep them safe.

Her father was waiting on the front lawn when they arrived. She waved to him from inside the car, but he just shook his head and stared at the ground. He didn't bother to approach them or offer to help them with their bags. Normally, he would have shoved Nathan to one side and lifted all five pieces of luggage at once. Her father said nothing as Nathan popped the trunk and lifted the bags one by one, stared off in the distance and muttered something under his breath that Chloe couldn't quite catch. As they made their way toward the house, he moved forward, his foot dragging where he'd dropped a dumbbell on it several weeks ago.

He'd been warned to stop lifting such heavy weights, but still insisted on bench-pressing as much as three hundred pounds every day, even after suffering a massive heart attack two years before. But his days as a power lifter were long gone, the cardiologist had said. He'd been known as "The Big E" when he'd won the World's Strongest Man title three years in a row in the seventies. If he stopped lifting his muscles would atrophy, he insisted, and to prove how well-developed he was even at sixty-five, he wore red tank tops every day of the year, except for Christmas Day, when he always switched to green.

"It's a goddamn freak show," the Big E told Chloe as they stood at the front door. When she reached up to hug him, he squeezed her, his biceps flexing, the front of his tank top stained with sweat. She peered over his shoulder at the front of the house with the shades drawn. He released her and rubbed at the perspiration stain with one of his thick hands.

"Have you heard from Ruth?" she asked, but her father just shook his head and peeled a piece of tape from his thick fingers.

"I hope you've got lots of lines for me," the Big E told Nathan as he reached to open the door. "God knows I don't know what the hell to say."

The three of them stood there staring at the front door, Nathan squeezing Chloe's arm and holding his index cards in the other hand. She wished someone would say something—anything—to break her out of the moment, something that would stop the feeling that she was floating above her body, that her feet had somehow been lifted off the ground, her legs deadened below the knee.

"Don't worry, E," Nathan said finally, as Chloe's father pulled open the door. "I've got you covered."

She hoped he was right, she thought, as she stepped forward, but worried that some of the best lines had been lost on the expressway, flattened in a mass of traffic, all because of the search for the baby the homecoming queen had left behind in the locker room.

"He's in the basement," Aunt Chickie announced, lumbering forward to kiss first Chloe and then Nathan on the cheek. She wore magenta lipstick to match the trim on her enormous housecoat, a trait Chloe had admired as a girl but now saw as intolerably sad. She'd come to live with them when Chloe and Irv were kids, and since she'd had no children herself, she often saw herself as a second mother to them. Chloe had never really seen her that way; she wanted more of the mother she had, not from a stand-in. She loved Aunt Chickie, though, and as the years passed, Chloe often wished she'd taken more advantage of Aunt Chickie's presence in the house, which was a large one, and not only because of her size.

From the inside of her bra strap Aunt Chickie removed a wad of tissues she always kept there because of her perspiration problem. She mopped at her brow and touched Chloe's arm, her fingers hot and slippery.

"We think it's the best place for him right now," she said, lowering her voice. "No one will know he's there."

Chloe followed Aunt Chickie to the basement door, her father and Nathan trailing behind her. The housecoat twitched heavily between Aunt Chickie's thighs as she walked. Chloe imagined the rawness there, the constant chafing which Chickie swabbed with baby ointment as many as twenty times a day to stave off the pain. According to Chloe's mother, no amount of ointment could assuage the humiliation of getting in one's own way. Her mother had little sympathy for Aunt Chickie's discomfort.

"Chickie's always going on about her chafed legs," her mother had said one day at the kitchen table when Aunt Chickie got up to go to the bathroom. "Always slathering herself with Desitin. She doesn't know what hurting is," her mother had said with a sly look on her face. "She's never had children."

As they stood in front of the basement door, Chloe saw her father backing away, his fingers taped and ready for lifting. She thought of her father lying prone on the weight bench, the barbell wobbling in his hands as he fought to keep it suspended. To avoid going downstairs she could offer to spot him, though she knew she couldn't save him if the weights collapsed. She would just stand there helpless while her father lay pinned to the bench. Better to face an infantile Irv any day, she thought, than to risk watching her father with a barbell crushing his chest, the bar leaving a thick indentation in the skin above his tank top.

"Aren't you coming, Dad?" she asked, a little more eagerly than she meant to. But the Big E just shook his head and sank into the sofa, pulling at the v-neck of his tank top.

"I've already seen that boy as a baby once," he said. "I did my part. I'm not about to do it again."

Aunt Chickie led the way down the stairs, her body slightly tilted at an angle to allow room for her massive frame. Chloe could see the overhead light down below Aunt Chickie's head, the banister shaking as she gripped it with her right hand.

"Even though this is a dry run," Nathan whispered, gripping her arms from behind, "we should still know our lines cold."

Chloe kept her eyes on the thick bra strap peeking out from Aunt Chickie's housedress, the edges frayed with perspiration and age. If she focused on that strap, she thought, as she felt her feet touching the basement floor, she wouldn't have to see anything she didn't want to.

At the bottom, Aunt Chickie turned around and wiped at the corners of her mouth with the wad of tissues. Nathan moved his hands over Chloe's hips. She could feel his breath in her ear.

"Your mother's in there with him," Aunt Chickie whispered, leaning in close to Chloe. The smell of Desitin was overpowering. "We had a hell of a time getting him to sleep last night, but he must be down now. I don't hear anything back there."

She moved aside to allow Chloe to pass. When she didn't move, Aunt Chickie smiled, her teeth smeared with magenta lipstick.

"Go on," she said. "Go and see your brother."

As she stepped forward into the dimly lit room in the corner of the basement, Chloe felt only the pressure of Nathan's hand squeezing hers. She forced herself to walk forward, looking down to watch each foot advance, heel touching the pavement and then leaning forward to rest on the toe. Her mother's silhouette against the wall grew enormous, reaching, her hands throwing curved shadows. Chloe closed her eyes and let Nathan push her along until she felt her feet stop moving and heard her mother's voice coming low from the corner of the room.

Nathan let go of her hand and stepped ahead of her, his shoulders blocking her view. "Oh, Christ," he breathed, "Jesus Christ," and then her mother's muffled sobs filled the room. She wondered how long she could remain there with her eyes closed, how long it would take them all to notice she was refusing to look. Her mother reached forward and tugged at Chloe's sleeve.

"Look at him," her mother said, "look at what's happened to my boy."

Chloe had no choice but to open her eyes. At first she saw only the tiny feet covered in pale blue booties, a white sheet draped over a wicker bassinet she recognized from old photographs. A pastel blanket swaddled his head, curving over the tiny shoulders and up over the crown, her view of his face obstructed by the folds of the pastel blanket. She stepped closer, freeing herself from her mother's grip, and stood directly over him. Her mother came around the other side, reached down and eased the blanket from the top of his head.

"Oh, Ma," she heard herself say, "oh, my God."

His almost man-sized head lolled from side to side, long blue veins pulsing under his translucent scalp. Although his body had managed to regress to infancy, his head remained nearly the same size it had been in adulthood, producing an effect more horrible than even Chloe had imagined. The curls on the top of his head were gone, his features fine and baby-like, lost in the huge globe of his skull. When he opened his mouth to yawn, several adult-sized teeth poked from his gums. Large bubbles of spittle blew out his lips. His eyes flickered for a moment, the blueness masked by white film. Chloe stared down at the body dwarfed by his giant head, the pink cords of his neck stretched almost to bursting.

"Who's going to want him now?" her mother asked suddenly, reaching down to pull the blanket more tightly around his shoulders, as if the pastel stripes could somehow hide the enormity of his head. She turned to Chloe, her face red and streaked with tears. "Who's going to want my boy?"

For a long time Chloe and Nathan said nothing. Aunt Chickie pressed her way past them and wrapped a flabby arm around her sister, her bra strap slipping down over one shoulder. As she watched the two of them standing in the shadows, Irv's veiny head covered from view, Chloe thought of what her father had said on the front lawn. It was a freak show, she thought, and Irv was the star attraction. The wayward teeth loomed in her thoughts even after she closed her eyes, the terrible blue veins that no amount of blankets could hide.

Homecoming Queen Says Aliens "Swiped" Baby

Associated Press

Long Island, NY

Seventeen-year-old Darlene Mulholland of Greenleaf Point, Long Island, has maintained that aliens "swiped" the baby boy she delivered in the Sagamore High School locker room last Saturday afternoon.

Mulholland, who gave birth eight days ago to the infant minutes before being named homecoming queen at the Sagamore High football game, admits to having delivered the baby in the locker room without assistance.

Detectives arrested Mulholland at Memorial Hospital on charges of abandonment and reckless endangerment of a minor. Hospital officials say Darlene began screaming hysterically about alien abduction.

"I knew Josh (Mulholland's twenty-one-year-old brother) was into UFOs, but I never knew Darlene believed," said neighbor Scott Hamilton, captain of the Sagamore High football team, when he heard of Mulholland's claim. "I guess it shows you never really know what goes on in someone's family."

Authorities believe the infant might still be alive, though police and FBI agents would release no official statement except to say that alien abduction "is not a feasible possibility."

No official word has been announced about when a grand jury will be assembled or whether Mulholland will be charged as an adult.

Family members have remained in seclusion at the Mulholland home, where a blue ribbon has been placed on the front window with the words "Bring Back Bubba" (now believed to be the baby's nickname) emblazoned on the front of the house.

At Sagamore High, students have begun wearing shirts with alien emblems on them as a measure of solidarity.

Coaches and teachers have yet to decide whether Mulholland will be disqualified as homecoming queen once charges are filed.

Chloe and Nathan sat silently at the kitchen table while the Big E poured whiskey into tall glasses with Spider-Man cartoons stenciled on the sides. Irv had always loved Spider-Man because of his lean red body and webs shooting out of his hands. When they were kids Chloe had argued that Spider-Man had no real superpowers, that his webs were mere gimmicks, fancy displays to distract his opponents rather than dazzle them with true superhuman strength or otherworldly device. Superman was heroic, she said, with his heaving chest and muscled arms, the shock of black hair that dipped down over his forehead. What did Spider-Man have but a lanky body and lifeless white eyes, a rounded red skull and a notoriously missing mouth?

"Spider-Man is a nobody," Chloe would taunt, pressing her chest forward and standing with her hands on her hips. "Only babies like Spider-Man."

Once they'd come to blows when they were twelve and nine, Irv pinning her down on the floor, his knees straddling her waist while he screamed "Spider-Man Rules!" until she relented.

Later Irv taped a note to her door enumerating Spidey's powers:

1. He has strength proportionate to a house spider.
2. He inherited the swift speed of an arachnid and can even dodge bullets.
3. He has spider-grip, allowing him to climb walls.
4. He has spider-sense. He can sense danger.

Chloe had gone immediately to the dictionary to look up the words "proportionate" and "arachnid." She knew Irv had copied the words from a comic book, but because she knew how crazed her teasing about Spidey could drive Irv, she tore his note down and left him alone. Years later, whenever she thought of the incident, she felt that strange sense of floating in her head at the thought of the change in his pocket pressing hard against her hips. It was a testament to Irv's influence over all of them, she thought, as she sipped at the whiskey her father poured for her, that her mother had kept the Spider-Man glasses all these years.

Her father poured three glasses of whiskey and talked about Ruth. He didn't blame her at all for dumping Irv there, but hoped she'd come back just the same. To help him express himself, Nathan passed cards to the Big E which he delivered in a booming voice.

"Tell him to be a man," he said, shaking his fist, and, "Who the hell can blame Ruth for dumping him?" then, "Fuck Spider-Man!"

At this last one, he leaned over to Nathan and whispered, "You'd better not let Flo hear that."

Aunt Chickie stood in the doorway, shaking her head and periodically mopping her brow with the tissues from under her bra strap. Nathan clapped.

"You're a natural, E," Nathan said. "I could use a man like you at some of my parties."

The Big E laughed and then stopped himself. Chloe didn't know what she might have said if given the chance. Nathan passed her an index card with the word "BINGO!" scrawled across it. She slid it under the table and pressed it between her hands.

Chloe didn't see her mother come into the kitchen. She wasn't sure how her mother had always managed this, to slip by undetected especially when Chloe spent so much of her time looking for her. As a child, Chloe often searched for her mother's shadow on sunny days, afraid that it might suddenly disappear if she didn't keep constant watch. Her mother had a way of slinking into a room, of suddenly appearing, her manner of moving about stealthy, covert. Irv must have inherited the gift from their mother, she thought, though she herself did not have it. Chloe had always been an awkward sort, her limbs gangly and loose, wrists and arms flying into tables and chairs no matter how hard she tried to control them. But her mother walked like a woman floating. Even the shuffle of her feet made no sound.

Chloe watched as her mother sat down, noiselessly, and motioned to the Big E to pour some whiskey. He set the glass in front of her but spilled half of it on the table. Aunt Chickie reached forward to soak it up with her tissues, but Flo held a hand in the air to stop her.

"That boy is in real trouble," she said. "I don't know what we're going to do for him now."

Nathan scribbled on one of the cards and sent it sailing across the table toward her when no one responded.

She turned the card over and raised her eyebrows at Nathan, shoving the card back in his direction.

"Maybe if Ruth had taken better care of my boy, this wouldn't have happened," she said. "Have you thought about that?"

Chloe lit a cigarette and swallowed some of her whiskey.

"Now, honey," Aunt Chickie said, laying a thick hand on her sister's shoulder, "that's not really fair now, is it? Ruth's been a very good wife to Ralph. You know that's true."

Flo tilted her shoulder to shrug off Aunt Chickie's hand. The Big E sighed and poured himself more whiskey. Chloe blew rings of smoke at the ceiling while Nathan wrote furiously on his cards. He passed one card to her, and she took a long drag on her cigarette before deciding whether to deliver the line.

LET'S NOT PLAY "LET'S BLAME RUTH," the card read. WHY NOT PLAY BINGO INSTEAD?

"Nathan's right, you know," she said, not looking at her mother as she spoke. "Someone's got to try to find Ruth. She's pregnant and alone, and something could happen to her."

Flo reached into her pocket and removed a spool of black thread and twirled it in her fingers. She'd worked for years at a fabric store and knew the thread count for any fabric imaginable. From time to time, Chloe wished she could consult her mother on fabric choices for her Bingo Ladies' dresses, but all her mother had ever done with her talent for sewing was to make custom unitards for the Big E's tournaments and Spider-Man appliqués for Irv's bed sheets when he was a boy. She'd pore over the comic books Irv bought at comic book stores and then would draw patterns for all of the different Spidey incarnations— a black cotton figure with a large white spider emblazoned on the chest, a red nylon Spidey dressed in blue leggings and a matching red hood with white netting for the eyes, and a one-piece red-clad Spidey with webbing drawn onto the fabric on swirls of black ink.

Chloe stubbed her cigarette out in the ashtray and thought of Irv lying there in the bassinet with his giant head, teeth poking from his sore gums, booties kicking at the air. If Ruth has any sense at all, she'd have run as far as she could. But she'd never learned to drive, and after all, she'd married Irv. She could not have gone far.

"Maybe Ruth can help him," she said softly, "and someone's got to look for her. And you do want him back, don't you?"

The Big E poured more whiskey into Chloe's glass, but she didn't drink it.

"It's time for his feeding," her mother said, as if not hearing Chloe's question. "The boy is hungry all the time, and I've got to get him on a schedule. We've got to have a routine."

Chloe offered no response as her mother got up from the table and headed back to the basement. She reached across the table for her pack of cigarettes to have something to do with her hands while Nathan stooped over his index cards, his Cross pen in hand.

"I guess that means she wants him the way he is," he sighed. "I can never figure out what your mother really means."

Her elbow crashed against his arm as Nathan wrote. His whiskey glass tumbled in front of Chloe and shattered, spilling whiskey all over the index cards. No one said anything as she jumped from the table, using the crumpled cards to scoop up pieces of glass. When Nathan reached over to help her up, she stared down at a sliver that had embedded itself in her hand, a stenciled piece of webbing stark against the opening in her flesh. She heard the Big E asking if she was all right as Nathan led her out of the room. Before they could make it to the bathroom where she would watch the blood spiral down the drain, she turned back toward the kitchen and forced herself to smile as she looked down at the one index card Nathan had managed to rescue.

"Spider-Man sucks," she read, and even though she wasn't sure he heard, she could have sworn she saw a smile playing at the corners of her father's lips.

Aunt Chickie wanted Chloe taken to the local hospital and stitched. She'd seen blood gush from Chloe's forehead when she was five. Irv had left one of Spider-Man's plastic foes balanced precariously on his dresser, and the sword wound up impaling Chloe right above the eyebrow.

"This girl's a bleeder," Aunt Chickie said, smearing her lipstick with the back of her hand. "I've seen it firsthand."

"No, no, I'll be all right," Chloe said, shaking her head and holding her arm out while Nathan tore paper bags into thin strips and held them to the cut in her palm. "It's just a little cut, that's all."

But Chickie insisted that the Big E examine the cut with his reading glasses on. He pressed his taped fingers to Chloe's hand and squeezed, the blood blossoming through the brown paper. She leaned into Nathan and closed her eyes against the pain. Her father could be unintentionally rough from all the years of power lifting.

"That's a deep cut," he said, "you should have it looked at," but before Chloe could respond, the room filled with the sound of an infant's screams.

Aunt Chickie hurried toward the basement, wheezing heavily. She grabbed Nathan by the arm and pulled him with her, leaving newly scattered index cards in their wake. As Nathan swung open the door, the screams became louder, her mother's voice hoarse beneath the wailing.

"I can't lift him by myself," her mother called, "somebody come and help."

For a minute Nathan stopped as Aunt Chickie's body pounded on the first step. Chloe could see the words forming in his mind even as he stood there holding on to the sopping mass of cards.

"Come and help him!" her mother called. "Someone help my boy!"

Nathan lifted Chloe's bloody palm to his lips, kissing the brown paper gently.

"Go find Ruth," he said, "I can handle this," and bounded down the steps, the banister rattling with his weight.

She imagined them cooing to Irv in unison, her mother humming bars of the old Spider-Man cartoon theme. Nathan's soft hands cradling the bulbous head, his fingers gripping the neck as they shifted him in the bassinet.

"Chloe, where's Chloe?" she heard her mother call. Bits of brown paper flaked away from the redness of her flesh, the lines in her palm crusted with blood. She thought she would faint for a minute and steadied herself by resting a hand on the wall, gray circles forming in her eyes. Without a word she turned away and headed toward the kitchen and sat down at the table sipping whiskey and smoking cigarettes. Vaguely she heard her mother call her name again, but she suddenly felt as if her insides had been emptied out, and that when no one was looking, someone had stuffed her with wads of cotton, the hole in her hand causing pieces of her to fall away bit by bit.

Once the sound of Irv's cries quieted down, Chloe took her keys and purse from the kitchen table and went into the Big E's trophy room. Since his retirement from power lifting, it had evolved into little more than a simple room with wood paneling and pictures on the walls, trophies on the shelves, and the Big E's weight bench in the middle of the floor. In his prime, the room had been the Big E's sanctuary. When he wasn't away on tournaments, he would often sit for hours polishing his trophies with special cloths and watching himself flex in the large mirror that hung on the wall. Weights and barbells now littered the floor once covered in a thick red carpet. Few people ventured into the room these days. Flo claimed that the clanging of barbells gave her migraines.

Chloe wondered if Nathan would stay in the basement all day with her mother, if he were cushioning Irv's head with his hands while her mother kept the bottle tilted for optimum sucking. At least Nathan was willing to help her mother, she thought with a sigh as she lit a cigarette with matches she found in the pocket of her jeans. Her mother had looked so worn, the circles under her eyes darker than she'd ever seen them, her mouth drawn. All her life, she'd tried to watch her mother as closely as she could, but still, she'd never been able to see her clearly. Her mother seemed to move in and out of focus as if seen through a movie projector with a cloudy lens. Just when she thought she'd managed to sharpen the picture, her mother seemed to dart out of the frame of Chloe's vision.

In the corner hung an eight-by-ten glossy of her father with a refrigerator strapped to his back, she and Irv cheering from the corner. A fan had snapped it for her father and had mailed it to them anonymously. She stood up and removed the photo from the wall, exhaling smoke over their faces. Irv couldn't have been more than nine with his Buster Brown shoes and Spider-Man T-shirt. Even then he seemed younger, his brown eyes shy and full of liquid while she smiled into the camera in her plaid jumper, their father's trademark platinum flat-top wilting slightly from the weight of the refrigerator balanced on a heavy metal contraption strapped to his waist and arms.

When he was a boy, Irv had imagined himself as Peter Parker, Spidey's alter ego, and had gone through a stint of taking photos of

Chloe and the others whenever possible. Flo had bought him a camera with a zoom lens at a secondhand shop, a fact which had unnerved Chloe even then. He often shot her from across the room when she was eating a sandwich or watching television. She could never be sure when he'd snap her. Once, because Irv had begged, Chloe had posed for him in a polka-dot dress and a floppy hat, smiling to show off her missing front teeth.

Later, Irv had come to feel disdain for poor orphaned Peter Parker, and her mother crated all the photos he'd taken as a child. Chloe wondered what had become of them, if somewhere her face had been crumpled in a sea of worthless mementos along with Irv's camera, tossed into a box filled with unsatisfactory book reports and smudged homework assignments.

Now she hated being photographed, agreeing reluctantly when Nathan pleaded with her or when fans asked her to pose next to the array of Bingo Lady dolls at shows. But at six she'd looked straight into the camera while the Big E sweated in his unitard, smiling at Irv with a camera around his neck.

She was about to hang the photograph back on its hook when her father appeared in the doorway. He smiled briefly and nodded at the picture, running his hand over the neckline of his red tank top. When Irv became a teenager, her father had dragged him along on tournaments to "beef" him up. He'd had difficulty doing even ten-pound curls, much to the Big E's dismay. Why did anyone need to lift weights, she once heard Irv ask their mother, when Spidey had so much more than muscle to make him strong? Spidey didn't need to work out to be a hero.

The Big E ran a hand through his flat-top, the platinum hair dye giving way to his own graying brown years ago after a scare with Clairol. The years of dye had made his scalp pulse with rawness, his vanity finally forced to give way under the constant threat of eczema.

I can no longer look the camera in the eye, she thought of telling him. *Unless I am Esther Bing.*

"I always knew he'd find a way to get back," the Big E said after a long silence, his voice gruff. "Even after he went off and got married, found himself a nice girl like Ruth, I told your mother, 'Don't think for a minute we've seen the last of that boy in this house.'"

Her father's sayings had always been endearing, whether he'd made them up himself or not. "You're so full of shit your eyes are brown," he'd say, or "Better to be pissed off than pissed on." He was a no-nonsense kind of man. The cut in her hand began to throb, tiny stabs of pain that started in the palm of her hand and moved upward toward her wrist. She wanted to light another cigarette but suddenly felt so tired, a fatigue that spread even through her lungs.

"I don't know where I went wrong," her father said softly, shaking his head at the hundreds of trophies and ribbons hanging on the walls, the rows of barbells stacked on the carpet. "Between you and me, that boy has always put a hair up my ass. All he ever cared about were those goddamned comic books, no matter how many times I tried to show him how to bench-press or lectured him on the need for vitamin supplements."

The Big E stood up and walked to the door. The muscles that had once been so prominent in his neck and shoulders now seemed to sag, as if the weight of Irv's infancy had dragged down every muscle in her father's body.

"You go on and find Ruth," he said. "If he can't come back for that baby, then what the hell is he going to come back for?"

She watched as the Big E lay back against the bench, puffing his chest out for a lift.

"Look at that girl in all the papers, that goddamned homecoming queen," he said, as he took in a deep breath and pushed the weights up in a series of presses. He let the bar fall back on the bench struts and sat up. "She left her kid, and look at where she is now."

Chloe turned to go, and then took one last look at her father before closing the door behind her. His brow was furrowed, beads of sweat forming in the V of his tank top. She felt a stab of pity for all of them—for her mother, for Nathan for having to bear the weight of her family, for Aunt Chickie and her chafed legs, for the homecoming queen, and even for Irv, though by all accounts, she had no reason to be sorry for him.

She made a list of places to try to find Ruth: a nearby shopping center, the comic book store, a donut shop, and last, though she hated to go there, Ruth and Irv's home. After all, a woman in Ruth's position had few places to go. She was eight months pregnant and unable to walk very far, and since she'd never learned to drive, for reasons no one really knew, she was limited to where she might be able to go. Her own parents had died some time ago, and she'd been raised by an aunt who had now been relegated to a nursing home which Ruth rarely visited. Irv, apparently, liked Ruth's aunt because her name was May—the same name as the aunt who had raised the orphaned Peter Parker—and Chloe believed that had been one of the reasons that he'd married Ruth. If anyone was going to get him out of the house at the age of thirty-three, it had to be a woman who somehow, at least in Irv's mind, had some connection to Spider-Man.

First Chloe drove by the comic book store where Irv worked, though she did not go in, just slowed the car down to peer through the plate glass window. A giant inflatable Spider-Man hung in the window, and cardboard cutouts of Superman and Spidey's arch enemy, the

Green Goblin, stood on either side of him. When she saw the store owner cast a glance toward the parking lot, Chloe sped away.

Next she tried the donut shop that she'd heard Ruth talk about several times, and then she drove to a strip mall near their house that featured a popular baby store. She parked the car near the entrance and walked inside, where she pretended to be looking at sleepers and layette sets while scanning the store for Ruth.

A woman in glasses and a smock with the store logo on it quickly approached her.

"Are you looking for something in particular?" the woman asked, smiling. "We have sleepers in every color of the rainbow and with just about any pattern you can imagine."

Chloe smiled back and shifted the hangers back in place.

"Well, yes, I am," she said, then blushed. "I mean, no, not exactly. We don't know what we're looking for just yet."

The woman laughed and glanced at Chloe's stomach.

"Oh, of course, that's always the way in the beginning," she said. "How far along are you?"

At first Chloe wasn't sure what the woman meant, then smiled and tapped at the flatness of her belly.

"Oh, no, it's not for me," she said, feeling her breath become shallow. "It's just that, the baby—well, no one seems to know how big this baby is right now."

The saleswoman gave Chloe a puzzled look and then tugged at the sides of her smock. "I see," she said, though it was clear that she didn't.

The woman busied her hands in the racks of clothes, hangers clattering as she moved them from side to side.

"You don't happen to be one of those people shopping for that missing baby, are you?" she asked. "We've had floods of people buying outfits for that baby. What's his name? Bubba. That poor Bubba. We've had people from all over the county buying outfits for a baby that girl didn't care about in the least. People have been more than generous where that girl's concerned, if you ask me."

"Darlene," Chloe said. "The girl's name is Darlene."

The saleswoman narrowed her eyes and turned away. She held up a blue jumper with rubber soles at the feet and a tiny blue hat to match.

"I'm not sure the hat will fit," she said. "People are saying he had a really big head. But this one is on sale."

Chloe took the outfit from the woman and decided to buy it, even though she'd had no intention of shopping for the homecoming queen. But the woman's indignation had irritated her. Who was she to know what the homecoming queen, or anyone else, for that matter, had suffered?

At the register she paid for the outfit with a credit card and waited for her receipt. As she was about to sign the sales slip, the young girl behind the counter looked at the signature on her credit card and then at Chloe.

"Chloe," she said. "That's a pretty name."

Chloe smiled and held the pen in her hand. She accidentally signed, "Esther Bing," and then crossed it out.

"I'm sorry," she said, crumpling the receipt in her hands, "but I've made a mistake with my name here." The girl gave her a puzzled look. "I mean, I just got married and signed my maiden name by mistake."

She forced a smile.

"I do that a lot," she added.

The girl tapped at a button on her computer and paged her manager to okay the second receipt. The manager initialed it, then glanced at the name and raised her eyebrows.

"Taft," the woman said, setting her reading glasses on the table to look at Chloe. "Do you know a Ruth Taft, by any chance?"

Chloe coughed and cleared her throat.

"Yes," she said, "she's my sister-in-law."

The woman nodded and reached under the countertop.

"She hasn't been in for a few days, and we have something she ordered." She bit her nails briefly and then held the large bag in her hands. "She said she'd be back to get this, and I was wondering if she'd had the baby."

The woman came around from behind the counter and handed the bag to Chloe.

"It was a very hard order to fill, and she's been waiting for this for some time," she said. "Frankly, the last time she came in, the other day, she wasn't looking well, and when I asked her what was wrong, she said she was concerned about her boy."

Chloe took the bags from the woman and thanked her.

"Is the baby all right? Her boy, I mean?" the woman asked.

"It's too soon to tell," Chloe said, "but we're hoping he will be."

The woman nodded gravely and pressed a hand on Chloe's arm.

"All these unwanted babies in the world," she said, shaking her head. "Just look at what's been in the papers. Please tell Ruth we're thinking of her. She's one of our best customers."

Chloe began to move toward the exit. The woman followed her and held the door for her.

"She's spoken of you, you know," the woman said. "She told us that you were a very good sister, and that you were one of the few people she could count on."

When Chloe didn't answer, the woman continued.

"It's very important to have a good sister, don't you think?" the woman asked.

Chloe nodded and fought to swallow.

"I'll make sure she gets these," she told the woman. "And I'll tell her you asked about her boy."

The woman smiled and waved as Chloe made her way out to the car. She opened the trunk and deposited the bags inside, turning to wave to the woman one last time before the woman closed the door and headed back inside. When she was sure no one was looking, she opened the bag to see what was in it. At first she found nothing surprising: packages of baby blankets and Onesies, different colored pacifiers. But on the bottom, she found what she knew had been there all along—dozens of infant stretchies in red and black with matching caps, all decorated with spiders on them.

Her last visit was to the Knights of Columbus where Irv, Ruth, and Flo had played bingo on Wednesday nights. It was a Tuesday, and Chloe was not expecting to find her there, already feeling the dread creeping through her at the thought of having to go to Irv's house. Since she and Irv rarely spoke, she'd only visited the house once for a dinner party Ruth threw for the family. After having to sit across from Irv for over an hour, Chloe complained of stomach cramps, and she and Nathan had driven home as fast as they could. They'd almost sideswiped a Jaguar in the left lane, but Chloe had been so desperate to get home, she'd never complained to Nathan about his driving.

There, sitting on a folding chair near the front of the hall, sat Ruth. She didn't stir when Chloe came in, and didn't look up until Chloe took the seat beside her.

"Ruth," she said, "Ruth, honey, are you all right?"

She finally turned to Chloe after a long pause and wrapped her arms around her. Her breath smelled of sour milk and cough syrup, and she wore a ratty T-shirt with the word "Baby" stenciled on the front.

"I should have known this was coming," Ruth said finally. "I don't know how I could have been so blind."

Chloe ignored the "No Smoking" sign and lit a cigarette. She wondered if Nathan were cradling Irv in his arms as they spoke, resting the heavy head in the crook of his arm.

"I caught him near the crib, you know," Ruth said, her voice trembling. "I had just come from the store and I was about to put the Onesies I bought into the new dresser we bought for the baby—you know, the cute little underwear with the snaps between the legs—I can't tell you how many times I've imagined snapping those little Onesies—and there he was with one leg swung over the side, trying to climb right in, almost like he couldn't help himself."

Ruth began to cry, wiping her tears with the back of her hand. Smoke burned in Chloe's lungs, her throat aching and raw.

"My God, Ruth," Chloe said, "what in the world did you do?"

For a long moment Ruth said nothing, just sat sniffling with her hands clasped over her belly. She stood up suddenly, clutching at her stomach as if afraid it might fall away if she suddenly let go.

"I looked away," she whispered. She turned her face toward the back door and leaned forward, as if wanting nothing more than anything to run, but not having the strength to do so. "I dropped the Onesies and pretended I didn't see."

Chloe pressed the brown paper into the slice in her hand until it began to bleed again. The blood swept over her palm, coloring the lines like webs.

She helped Ruth out to the car and settled her into the passenger seat, even buckling her seatbelt for her. Ruth hung her head and wiped at her nose as Chloe pulled out of the parking lot.

For a while they sat in silence until Ruth began humming a tune Chloe didn't recognize at first, but then she realized it was the same song that Irv had hummed all those nights when they were teenagers and drove home after bingo games with their mother. The theme song to the Spider-Man cartoon that Chloe and Irv had sung when Chloe was still Chloe and not Esther Bing, and Irv was still just her brother, a little boy named Ralph who watched Spidey with her on Saturday mornings.

Later, after she'd brought Ruth back to the house and she'd refused to look at her infantile husband, Chloe sat out on the back porch with Ruth in the dark. They sat side by side in old wicker chairs and watched the smoke drifting up in clouds toward the moonlight coming through the porch window. If she closed her eyes, Chloe could almost pretend she was home again surrounded by her Bingo Ladies, their fabric bodies silhouetted against the night sky. In those moments she was Esther Bing, renowned dollmaker. She wondered if Ruth knew that the Irv in Chloe's dreams was no baby, and that at night she sometimes held her Bingo Ladies to her chest and squeezed them until the armatures bent, until there was nothing but cigarette smoke and the smell of cotton batting on her hands, a whole synthetic world.

At her first doll convention, Chloe met Gloria Rollins near the vending machines. She'd been admitted to the doll organization, NIADA, on the strength of Polly's Large Picture Frame, a doll with tight foam curlers at her brow and a lollipop stick cigarette between her wrinkled lips. The room was lined with long narrow tables, dolls with Rastafarian hair and hippie dolls with rainbows on their chests covering every inch. Chloe wore a name tag with "Esther Bing" printed on it and had walked down the aisles slowly, nodding at the other dollmakers with a pack of cigarettes stuffed in her breast pocket.

"So," Gloria had said as they waited for their candy bars to fall into the slot on the bottom, "does Polly win or lose?"

Chloe laughed and followed Gloria to the lounge where the doll-makers "dished the dolly dirt," as they called it. It was the first time she'd introduced herself as Esther Bing, and with Gloria in a huge muu-muu covered with rag dolls that she often threw to others across the room, Chloe felt comfortable enough to tell Polly's story.

Polly felt like a lucky woman even when she didn't win, Chloe explained, biting a piece of her chocolate bar. She didn't blame anyone for her husband's running off with the catechism teacher or for the wrinkles that had appeared in her neck at thirty-five. She'd once had a terrible crush on a priest and had snuck behind the altar after Mass to sip at his chalice. Her best friends were bingo players, and they went every week to a different game, never chancing the same caller twice.

"But does she win the large picture frame?" Gloria asked, stopping to throw the candy wrapper in the trash behind them. "That's the prize, isn't it?"

And when Chloe explained that "the picture frame" referred to a bingo that framed the card, that cash was always the prize, they laughed and pounded the table until the other dollmakers stared at them.

Later Gloria tried to convince Chloe to approach dollmaking as an enterprise, and that the best way to market her product was to imagine herself as a doll—even to dress like one, as Gloria did. She urged Chloe to dye her hair a flaming red and to fashion a huge bingo card out of oaktag to wear around her neck at doll shows while Gloria called out numbers.

"Like a walking, talking Bingo Lady," Gloria had said, though Chloe just smiled and passed on the idea.

Gloria had raised four children and weathered three divorces by making dolls. She believed in encouraging people to play with her dolls at conventions, to touch them the way they had stroked their baby dolls as children. Chloe couldn't bear the thought of some rich housewife squeezing Polly's curlers or pawing at the curled horse hair of her graying bangs. It was bad enough to imagine Polly being left by a bay window to emphasize the rings around her neck, her body turning pale and sun-streaked.

"I don't like them to be touched," she told Gloria, her face flushing at the revelation. "They can look at them, but really, my dolls are not meant to be touched, not like that."

Gloria nodded and placed one of the rag dolls stitched to her muumuu in Chloe's warm hands.

Later, when Chloe's Polly won third prize in the cloth doll category, Gloria had come up to her at her booth and pumped her hand up and down.

"Well, I guess Polly's brought you luck," she said.

Chloe fingered the bingo card in Polly's raised hand, not bothering to explain that Polly didn't believe in luck. Bingo, to Polly, like most things, was preordained. Just like life, the fix was in.

When Nathan finally came to bed, Chloe tied a knot in the terry cloth robe that she always wore whenever she slept in that room. Her mother had long since converted her old bedroom into a sewing room, with spools of thread scattered across the bureau, and bibs with the stitching only half-finished piled on top of an old wicker basket. In her adolescence the room had been covered with daisies her mother had carefully cut from a wallpaper pattern and glued haphazardly around Chloe's bed. The centers of the daisies were lemon yellow, and though they'd once been her favorite flower, Chloe began to feel that the centers of the daisies had become eyes that bored into her skin. After she'd gone off to college, she'd prevailed upon her mother to tear down the

daisies and to paint the room a stark white, but not to hang family pictures or framed needlepoint, to leave the walls bare. Oddly she'd hon-
ored Chloe's request, though only because Irv's room remained covered
with Spider-Man stencils frayed at the edges, his baby pictures tucked
in every available corner.

"I don't know which is worse, Irv's screaming or the clichés,"
Nathan said. "I'm blocked. No matter what I do, I just can't seem to
come up with an original line."

He sighed heavily and rolled toward her. From beneath his pillow,
he plucked the index card where he'd written their questions about Irv
the day they'd left. He held the card up for them to read the questions
together, tracing his finger over the ink that his Cross pen had so finely
etched on the card.

"Well, we know the answer to number one just from one look at his
head," he said. "And he's definitely crying out for his mother." He
crossed out the first two questions and then looked at Chloe. "What do
you think about numbers three and four? I can't tell what's going on in
that head of his, whether he willed this or not."

Chloe stared at the questions and then turned her face away.

"I don't know," she said. "I've never understood anything Irv has done."

Nathan nodded, slid the card back under his pillow, and set the
Cross pen carefully on the bedside table. He kissed her forehead and
breathed into her hair.

"You should get some sleep," he said, wrapping an arm around her
waist. "We're all supposed to start pitching in tomorrow, I heard your
mother say so. 'Many hands make easy work,' she said." Nathan sighed
again. "You can see what I'm up against."

Chloe loosened the knot in her robe.

"All of us?" she asked. "What do we have to do?"

He didn't look at her as he spoke.

"'Wipe his ass,' is what the Big E told us," he said, trying to hold in his laughter. "He's the only one with anything good to say. Today I gave him a line, and he even improvised," Nathan said. "It was all I could do not to applaud."

They lay together like spoons. With Nathan there, the room didn't seem quite so dark.

"I can't get the words down fast enough," he whispered, drawing a hand over her robe. "As soon as I have a chance to write something down, your mother's singing some lullaby or talking in nursery rhymes. I can barely get a word in."

He threw an additional index card he found under the blanket across the room and closed his eyes. Chloe tried to concentrate on the rhythm of her breath and the feel of his arm wrapped tightly over her middle. *I am Esther Bing, I am Esther Bing*, she said over and over to herself until at last her head and body seemed to be one again and she didn't have to pinch at her leg to remind herself that this was her body, and that no one could hurt her, not while she was Esther Bing.

DA to Mulholland: Bad Brownie

Associated Press

Long Island, NY

District Attorney Sandra Madreski expressed outrage that Mulholland has been depicted in the press as "an innocent Girl Scout when she is nothing but a spoiled teenager who chose her crown over an innocent baby."

According to reports, Mulholland took great care to tie the cord off with shoe laces before cutting it with a pen knife she'd kept from her Girl Scout days, a fact which impressed even the police.

"This was no model scout," Madreski said, citing claims that Mulholland had been notoriously lazy at Brownie troop meetings.

Former troop leader Angela Romanoski said that she remembered Mulholland as an indolent child who had difficulty following the rules and was often tardy.

"She was always late and rarely wore her uniform," Romanoski remembered. "I was shocked to learn she'd gone on to Girl Scouts. She was a very bad Brownie."

Romanoski added that Mulholland's ability to cut the cord and abandon the infant could not be blamed on poor Brownie training, as sex education has never been part of the Brownies' teachings.

Friends of the Mulholland family report that Wendy Mulholland instilled the importance of Girl Scouts into her daughter and frequently drove Darlene door to door to sell cookies.

"She is shocked by what Darlene has done," commented one friend. "She just cannot imagine her very own daughter leaving that boy that way."

The Mulhollands have refused to offer any comment to the press, a fact which some friends attribute to their "grave disappointment" in Darlene.

In the morning Aunt Chickie hung an elaborate schedule of shifts marked in orange construction paper. Chloe posted the morning's article about the homecoming queen next to it and drew a circle around the headline. She was tempted to leave a plate of brownies at the table but realized no one would find this funny. Caring about anyone but Irv was selfish and misdirected, her mother would say, if Chloe had dared to press her. She shook her head and drew her finger across the photo of young Darlene in her Brownie uniform. Didn't these people have anything better to do, Chloe wanted to know, than to crucify a confused young girl?

Everyone would work in pairs, Aunt Chickie said, since two people were needed to lift Irv from the changing table to the wicker bassinet—one to support his giant head and the other to make sure his constant kicking didn't send him flying to the basement floor. The fact that he kicked showed some hope of resistance left in him, an indication that he might be trying to return, as if he were trying to bicycle his way home or flail his limbs in the face of his own infancy. They had to be very careful with him because the kicking made it seem easy to drop him. For a brief moment Chloe allowed herself to imagine the splat of his head cracking like a giant egg while she sang "Humpty Dumpty" at the top of her voice.

Chloe and Aunt Chickie had first shift, Aunt Chickie explained, because it was only fair to let Flo finally get some rest.

"My poor sister's been up night and day holding the bottle to his mouth," she said, stopping only when she saw the tears welling in Ruth's eyes. "Although of course that's nobody's fault."

Nathan and Ruth would take the afternoon shift, though it was generally agreed that Ruth would have little responsibility except to constantly speak into Irv's ear to urge him back. Nathan had written the specs the night before, he said, and had detailed instructions about what Ruth should and should not be allowed to say. She couldn't be expected to lift him in her condition, they agreed, as the obstetrician had warned that too much activity at this point in her pregnancy might bring about the breaking of her water. She was two centimeters dilated and ten percent effaced, he'd said on her last visit. The slightest shock might send her into labor before the thirty-sixth week. Ruth had of course agreed not to tell her doctor about this particular shock, though who would have believed her anyway?

"Make sure you call him a 'man' at all times," Nathan told Ruth in a firm voice. "I've underlined the word 'man' in red ink. You can't miss it."

The Big E suggested that Nathan hold Irv's head to Ruth's belly while they pleaded with him to put an end to this nonsense.

"You let him know that baby in there is the only one that's welcome," the Big E said. He leaned forward on his elbows, his biceps bulging as he cupped one calloused hand over his mouth in case Flo should overhear. "Time to pull himself up by his goddamned boot straps—or booties, or whatever the hell he's wearing these days. Time to be a man—just like Nathan says—and get on with it."

But Ruth seemed not to be listening, stroking her belly and humming the Spider-Man theme low in her throat.

Only the Big E had a solo shift, with Flo and Nathan taking the overnight. The Big E was strong enough to handle Irv on his own, and Nathan had agreed to a double shift. He had the most energy, everyone agreed, and he seemed to be the only one who ever knew what to say.

"The main thing is for all of us to try to get him back," Aunt Chickie added, the coasters under the chair creaking under her weight. "The boy—I mean, man—has got to come to his senses."

Chloe wanted to ask when Irv had ever been known to have any sense, but instead she gripped the edges of the table and forced herself to stand. She walked slowly toward the refrigerator with the carton of milk in her hand. As she stared at the schedule and at the photos of the homecoming queen taped on the door, she couldn't help but think of her mother hovering over Irv, her face and arms sticky with drool, Desitin and powder staining her blouse.

"I want to switch," Ruth said suddenly, pulling herself up from the chair and waddling over to Chloe. She'd changed the ratty "Baby" t-shirt but her face looked unwashed, her belly seemed to have expanded overnight. "I want to be on Chloe's shift."

She threw her arms around Chloe, the milk carton shaking in Chloe's hand as she tried to hold on to it. She reached out to steady herself, her hand falling against the homecoming queen's face, tearing the photo at the corners and sending the article to the floor.

"It's all right, Ruth, it's all right," Chloe said, easing backward to set the carton on the table. "You can be on my shift."

"Oh, no, she can't," Flo shouted from the bedroom. "She stays right where she is."

At the sound of Flo's voice they all froze. Ruth's belly pushed awkwardly against Chloe's middle, twitching as if it wanted to avail itself of Ruth's body but couldn't. Chloe hadn't heard her come upstairs and wondered how she managed to move about the house so quietly. Her mother had been in the basement since Ruth's return, and as far as Chloe could tell, she hadn't spoken to Ruth at all.

Flo stood in the doorway with a bundle of red fabric in her hands and a teething ring between her teeth. She didn't look at Ruth when she spoke but instead directed her gaze right at Chloe.

"She left that boy here, and now she'll do whatever we say to get him back," she said through gritted teeth. "If she hadn't left my boy, maybe he'd be back by now."

Ruth began to weep. Aunt Chickie handed her a ball of tissues from her bra strap, but Ruth waved a hand in the air to refuse them. Chloe stood up calmly and shielded Ruth with her body.

"That's not fair," she said. "You know that is not fair."

Nathan slipped the Big E a card, and he slammed his fist on the table.

"For Christ's sake, Flo," he shouted, "Cut the goddamned cord!"

No one said anything as her father stormed out of the room, not even when the barbells started to crash, one loud clang after another. Chloe heard her parents screaming through the walls, their warbled voices punctuated by curses. She sat down next to Ruth and held on to the sides of the table to steady herself as Aunt Chickie headed toward the trophy room. She shouldn't have said anything, Chloe thought, feeling the cool wooden table beneath her fingers. She should have kept quiet, the way she always had.

"Why can't I be on your shift?" Ruth asked.

She pawed at the white circle where her wedding ring had been before she'd swollen up with pregnancy and the burden of having an infant husband.

"Because I am Esther Bing, and I should have never brought you back," she whispered, though Ruth seemed not to be listening. She wondered how Nathan could continue writing through the racket. His pen never stopped.

Just then she heard the cries coming from the basement, sharp staccato bursts of air.

Ruth squeezed Chloe's arms, her fingernails leaving white marks in Chloe's flesh.

"What do I do?" Chloe asked, but before Ruth could answer, Aunt Chickie came rushing toward her, magenta lipstick bleeding the sides of her mouth.

"It's our shift," Chickie said, and then they were heading toward the basement door. The stairway seemed to grow more narrow with every step down. If she could just pretend he was a doll, Chloe thought, if she could make herself believe that inside Irv's body was nothing but tightly coiled balls of fiber fill, she could do this. She would force herself to imagine he were made out of nylon and painted cotton, like the one baby doll she'd made years ago, before the Bingo Ladies had come to her in dreams, first one and then in groups—Dora with Four Corners, Greta and Her Blotters, Daisy Mac's Jackpot, Lady Smokers in Back Row. The baby doll had won a prize. She'd called it Jeffrey: Sunday Morning Feeding with his carefully stuffed feet and painted carrot juice dribbling from his bow mouth.

The doll was early work, unpracticed, with his loose diaper and booties, a pair of lopsided ears. Still, he'd brought her praise from young mothers who mingled with the real collectors at the annual doll show at the Coliseum. Such detail in the tiny feet, right down to the minia-ture toenails, one mother had said, made Jeffrey seem so lifelike she could almost hear him breathing. The woman had bought the doll for three hundred dollars and told Chloe she'd be a natural mother some-day when she had children of her own with mouths plugged with pacifiers and sticky clapping hands.

A thick blue bonnet covered Irv's head. Her mother had hastily sewn the bonnet the night before to obscure his enormous head from view. Not that it helped, but her mother had tried. The crying filled the room, high-pitched and nervous. Was he practicing his crying, Chloe wondered, as she followed Chickie to the changing table littered with diapers, Wet Ones, and bottles soaking in warm water. Irv had always loved to rehearse. As a kid he'd practiced dialogue from each weekly Spider-Man cartoon, until he could recite both the Green Goblin's and Spider-Man's lines without a single mistake. When she'd told him he didn't have the right inflection for a good Spider-Man, that even in adolescence his voice was too high-pitched, he'd retreated to his room and slammed the door.

"That's the way Spidey talks!" he screamed. "What do you know about Spidey?"

Chickie bustled about the room, gathering up the bottles and diapers.

"I'm afraid I don't know his cries well enough yet," Aunt Chickie said nervously. "What do you think he wants?"

Chloe shrugged, trying hard to maintain her composure as Aunt Chickie untied the knot in his bonnet. He's a doll, Chloe told herself, closing her eyes and trying to imagine the giant head shrinking down into a perfect sphere she could shape and stuff, paint a smiling face with a horsehair brush. She thought of the way the dolls came to her, offering their stories, their preferences in men and lipstick, their long-held grudges against brothers and sisters. One doll, Rosalee, had been cross with other bingo players and cursed the jackpot winners under her breath; Sadie thought her luck had run out until she'd fallen in love with the caller.

She vaguely heard Aunt Chickie saying her name while Irv squirmed in the bassinet, his mouth and gums overripe, as if they'd been festering in babyhood for too long. She felt her mouth go dry while her aunt's hands moved lower, her dimpled fingers poking awkwardly about his waist.

"I think he needs to be changed," her aunt said, because the smell suddenly hovered, thick and dank, like something rotting. "You've got to help me, Chloe," Aunt Chickie said suddenly, her voice cracking on the word "help." "You've got to hold him still."

Chloe reached down and pressed her hands against the sides of his head, the bald flesh surprisingly warm and pliable, as if she could peel it away with her fingernails one layer at a time.

"Don't let go of his head," Aunt Chickie reminded her. Chloe forced herself not to recoil, to stand there with her fingers bearing down on the pulse point in his temples. His feet moved frenetically in the air, the soft spot throbbing beneath the translucent skin. His cries persisted until Aunt Chickie's hands began to move all at once, pulling at the diaper as she spoke to him in a low voice, telling him how desperate they were to have him back.

Everything that happened afterward seemed to move in slow motion—the sharp rip of the diaper tabs being torn open, the pasty feces, the sickly smell of Desitin. Chloe would not look, she told herself, keeping her face averted, as Aunt Chickie lifted his bottom and slid the diaper away, his infantile maleness revealed. Yet she couldn't stop herself from staring at the raw testicles and flesh no bigger than a thumb.

"Help me get the diaper on," Aunt Chickie said sharply, sweat forming on her brow as she fought to secure the fresh diaper tabs. "All we need is for him to catch cold."

Chloe taped the sides of the diaper the way she'd watched so many of her friends do, checking the elastic around the legs for leaks. She had always been an obedient child. After all, hadn't her mother taught her that? And as the thought occurred to her, she could imagine her mother praising her for what a good job she'd done, how well she'd taken care of Irv. What a good sister she was.

Later, after she'd held the bottle up to his lips, she watched as Aunt Chickie smiled down at him, cooing silently, her magenta lips forming obscene shapes as she bent toward him. Tissues slipped from the sleeve of her house dress and floated to the floor.

"Yes, there you go, Ralph, come on now and be a big boy," her aunt said in a high-pitched voice. "You've got to be a big boy again. We're all counting on you."

No matter how much Aunt Chickie coaxed, Chloe would not join in.

"Nathan said to call him a man," Chloe said, but Aunt Chickie shushed her and went on prattling about how they all missed him, how he needed to come back if not for his own sake then for Ruth's.

"Have you forgotten, Ralphie?" Chickie asked, raising her voice ever so slightly. "You're not a baby anymore. Don't you want to be a big boy again?"

His eyes seemed to glaze over as Aunt Chickie spoke, his eyes darting back and forth as if forcing themselves not to focus. He blew bubbles of spit with his lips and farted.

"Go on, Chloe, say something to him," Chickie said when the smell of his gas drifted up from the bassinet. "Say anything. Maybe he'll listen to you."

For a brief moment Chloe did imagine him as a doll she'd made out of wire and strips of nylon, his head about to burst at the seams, long wiry hairs hanging awkwardly from his baby hands. She leaned down close and breathed in his ear. The tiny feet stopped kicking.

"Hey, Irv," she whispered, "what the hell do you know about Spidey?"

It was the end of her shift. She ran up the stairs as he began to squawk, out to the street and across to her parked car, fumbling in her pocket for the keys and reaching in blindly for one of the Bingo Ladies she kept hidden in the trunk. No one knew she kept a doll in there for emergencies, not even Nathan who thought he knew everything about her, who always knew just what to say. Even he didn't know how badly she needed the feel of a doll in her arms to be herself again. She held the doll tightly to her chest, the wires of the armature stabbing her rib cage. With her eyes narrowed, she focused on the name stitched in the back of the Bingo Lady's head. Harriet, Queen of the Quinella, a wooden bingo card glued to her nylon hand, the colorful chips forming the number seven across the length of the card.

The first time Irv came to her room at night, Chloe had thought it was the dog, Gretchen. They'd stayed out late at bingo with their mother, something they often did when the Big E trained for upcoming tournaments. Chloe had brought her own jar of pennies to mark her numbers on the wooden boards. She'd painted her name on the jar with glittery pink nail polish. She was thirteen and in love with her name. *Chloe*, she would tell the boys in her daydreams, *I'm Chloe*. The faceless boys held her hands and whispered in her ear. There wasn't anything they wouldn't do, they said, for a girl named Chloe. She stenciled her name above the daisies that surrounded her headboard and wore a gold name plate the Big E had given her for her thirteenth birthday. All the girls had them that year, but Chloe had always thought her necklace was the prettiest simply because she had the prettiest name.

Ralph was just Irv, she thought, as she fingered the necklace that rested at the base of her throat. But she was Chloe, a girl whose name promised she was going places, far away from comic books and Spider-Man cartoons. A girl named Chloe was meant for bigger things than the crashing sound of barbells and the sweaty air left behind by a brother who spent half his life in the bathroom.

Her mother carried a bag full of multicolored bingo chips and a magnetic wand to sweep them away—enough for all of them, she said. She didn't know why Chloe had to bring her own.

"Because she's got to write her name over everything," Irv said in the car as Chloe held the jar of pennies close to her chest. "Even her stupid pennies."

But she ignored him and smiled to herself at the sight of her name glowing in the darkness of the back seat. At sixteen his voice had yet to change and he had few friends, a fact Chloe often pitied him for. If he stopped reading comics and playing bingo with their mother, she often thought, he might have found himself a life.

They played bingo on Thursdays at the same Knights of Columbus where Irv and Ruth and her mother still played every week. Sometimes Chloe went along but didn't play, doodling her name instead in the margins of her notebook while her mother and Irv searched their cards for the numbers being called. Sometimes she begged not to go, to sit in the corner of the gym and watch her father's muscled neck bulging, his high platinum flat-top shining in the lights. But her mother always insisted that she join them, declaring bingo a family night and the gym full of hulking men no place for a young girl to be hanging about. Chloe liked to watch her father lift, but Irv preferred bingo.

"How's he ever going to learn to be a man," the Big E said one night while Chloe drew her name in bubble letters on yellow construction paper, "when all he does is listen to a bunch of blue hairs praying for a jackpot?"

On the night that Irv came into her room, Chloe was close to a jackpot. A layer cake, three bingos on every other line of the card. She felt lucky.

"All I need is G 53," she squealed, but Irv told her to shut up and have some respect for the other players.

What she remembered most about the night was not that the caller had reprimanded her for giggling or that the assistants told her mother no minors could win a jackpot, that her mother would have to collect Chloe's winnings, but that Irv kept shoving his hand into her jar.

"Stop taking my pennies," she said, when he reached in for another fistful. "These are mine."

But he just laughed and availed himself of them over and over again, no matter how many times she tried to pull them away or slapped at his hand.

"Mom, tell him to stop," she finally said, louder than she meant to, her voice echoing through the bingo hall. Her mother glared at Chloe but said nothing, the other players urging the caller to repeat the number no one had heard. Chloe felt her face burn as everyone turned to look at her. The caller cleared his throat.

"G 55," the caller said, and then a woman next to her in a flower print dress with heavy make-up and multicolored blotters strewn over the table jumped up from the table. She knocked Chloe's jar to the floor and shouted "Bingo!"

Chloe bent down to pick up the spilled pennies. One of the assistants held up the woman's card and read off her numbers.

"B 3, B 5, B 6, B 9, B 13, I 20, I 21, I 29 . . ."

And then, as she plucked the glass from her thumb, which surprisingly left no blood, she found the C and H split in two, the only piece that was left intact spelling out the word "loe."

"That's a good bingo," the caller said, and everyone applauded, even her mother and Irv, who often scowled all the way home when they didn't win.

As Chloe gathered up the remaining bits of glass, the woman next to her reached down to take her hand. She helped Chloe to her feet and clucked her tongue at the sight of the broken penny jar, not even turning to look at the man who was heading down the aisle with a palm filled with twenty-dollar bills. She smiled and smoothed a strand of hair behind Chloe's ear.

"Don't worry, dear," the woman said, as she must have seen the look on Chloe's face at the sight of the broken pieces of glass where her name had shone so prettily. "It's still a lovely name."

Chloe dumped the pennies and pieces of glass into a paper bag someone had left on the table for collecting trash at the end of the night. She glanced around the room for her mother and Irv, but they were lost in the crowd of bingo players headed out of the hall lighting cigarettes and grumbling about an inept caller. B 17 had come out three times that night, one man said with a cigar pressed between his lips. What were the chances? Chloe thanked the woman for her help and turned to go, but the woman stopped her.

"Just a minute," she said, leaning down to whisper in Chloe's ear. "I saw you waiting for G 53." She pressed a twenty-dollar bill into Chloe's hand. "Maybe this will bring you luck next time."

Before she could refuse the money, the woman turned on her heel to go, her blotters packed inside a crocheted box with her name on it.

Greta, it said, in bold yellow stitches, *Bingo Lady,* and Chloe smiled, thinking that Greta was the prettiest name she'd ever heard, second only to her own.

She didn't tell anyone about the Bingo Lady, just as she didn't tell anyone about the dream she thought she had that night of her covers bunched up at her waist, the elastic of her panties moving down below her rear, a cold finger poking its way between her legs. When she turned in the bed, she saw Gretchen standing at the door of her room, Spider-Man flashing by, the thud of the bathroom door closing. For a long time she wondered how the dog had managed to pull down her panties. She imagined Gretchen clenching the elastic band in her teeth like the dog in the Coppertone ad revealing the girl's striking white bottom while the girl craned her neck to look back. The next day Chloe asked her mother to fix the lock on her door, but her mother said they would have to wait for the Big E, who was leaving for a tournament the next day.

"Why do you want a lock?" her mother asked with a snort. "Your brother won't steal your pennies."

Chloe didn't answer, though the next night she thought of Greta as she fought to sleep. Carefully she slid the twenty-dollar bill in the waistband of her panties. She would feel the bill scratching her, she thought, if it were to move suddenly during the night. She didn't sleep at all, staring at the daisies surrounding her bed and her name above the bed painted in lilac. All night long the theme from Spider-Man blasted in her ears, though there was no television playing, only the sounds of the dog's nails clicking on the linoleum floor and her own shallow breath hissing through her open mouth.

Homecoming Queen Free on Bail: Bubba Still at Large

Associated Press

Long Island, NY

Darlene Mulholland, the homecoming queen of Sagamore High, was released today after her parents posted her $500,000 bail. She left the courthouse with her parents, Gerald and Wendy Mulholland, her older brother Josh, and her attorney, Lawrence Englebaum.

Mulholland refused to answer questions shouted at her by reporters demanding to know what had happened to the infant she delivered four days ago in the Sagamore High locker room.

Shouts of "Baby killer!" and "Bad Brownie!" could be heard above the crushing crowd of more than three hundred people outside the courthouse.

Mulholland still refuses to name the infant's father. Some of those close to the family have said that she has not revealed the father's name even to her own parents.

When asked by a reporter whether his client was indeed sane, referring to her earlier comment about a possible alien abduction, Englebaum issued a terse "No comment" as he ushered the Mulhollands into a waiting limousine.

Josh Mulholland, however, stopped at the door of the limousine and spoke to one reporter.

"A ten-pound kid came out of her?" he said. "It must have been some kind of alien. You know—a freak."

Neighbors say Wendy Mulholland has gone into seclusion and prays constantly for the return of baby Bubba, reciting the rosary as many as fifty times a day. Brother Josh appeared briefly at the front door and stared up at the sky.

In the car Chloe wrapped Harriet in a plastic bag, shoving newspaper clippings covered with the homecoming queen's face inside the bag when Nathan called her in to supper. She closed the trunk and forced a smile as Nathan stood watching her through the car window. Harriet had been one of the few dolls Chloe had refused to sell, perhaps because the doll had won several prizes. The doll had somehow maneuvered its way into Chloe's heart—something Chloe rarely allowed to happen—as soon as she'd finished needle-modeling her face. Harriet was the type of woman who sewed baptismal gowns for her grandchildren, and kept lucky pennies in her housecoat for admittance to heaven in case of sudden death. And she could predict a good bingo even before she had one.

The Big E was making his famous sloppy joes on oversized buns, Nathan told her, which he had always called "manwiches" in deference to an old 1970s commercial. They would sit down to a family meeting for which Nathan had already written an outline. Everyone was wound too tightly at this point to trust themselves to speak without prompts, he'd suggested. Ruth had taken to lying beside the bassinet and sobbing right after Chloe's shift.

"We could have used you in there, babe," Nathan said as he helped Chloe out of the car and explained what had happened while she was gone. "I was running out of lines for them to say. Nothing but food and silence in there now."

He lit Chloe's cigarette and watched as she blew smoke at the hood of the car. "I told your mother she's got a week at best to get Ralph to come around. 'You get someone in here,' I said, 'or else it's party time.'"

She dragged on the cigarette, the heat rising in her face and down her chest. Having parties was a waste of time, her mother said, unless they were for birthdays, which was the only holiday she could stand celebrating.

"I cannot for the life of me understand why anyone would shell out thousands of dollars for a silver anniversary or weddings on yachts," her mother liked to say. "Life is too short for streamers and party hats. Blow out your candles and get on with it."

At times Chloe wondered if her mother had become a closet Jehovah's Witness because of her sudden disdain for holidays. In the past few years she'd stopped going to midnight Mass and banned the Big E's annual stringing of lights in the front yard, a tradition that had once been a favorite of his. Holidays were for kids, she said, and hers were grown. No more need for Easter baskets or stockings, cookies for Santa Claus left on the mantel. She'd even taken to taping a frowning pumpkin on her door to ward off trick-or-treaters. Once Ruth became pregnant, Chloe waited for her mother's old exuberance to return, but Flo said that having a grandchild wouldn't change the way she felt.

"That baby will be Ruth's," her mother said. "Let her have the parties."

Of course her one concession was Irv's birthday, which she left to Nathan to plan every year, though it always contained a Spider-Man theme. Irv would feign surprise at the door, rushing in as they oohed and ahhed over the Spider-Man cake and plastic Green Goblin figures, the piles of gifts wrapped in Spider-Man paper. Every year they sat in straight-backed chairs while Irv opened his gifts, which inevitably disappointed him, although they were always practical and in good taste— crewneck sweaters and multicolored ties for his job at the comic book store, a gift certificate to dinner for him and Ruth. Their mother gave Irv the same thing every year: boxes of cotton briefs—his trousseau, she called it, as if she were forever sending him out into the world.

"God knows I need these," Irv would say, laughing, his face going crimson as he stuffed them back into the tissue paper.

When the party was over, Nathan would weave through traffic and flash his brights at anyone moving below seventy miles an hour while Chloe clung to the suicide strap above her seat. She never complained about his driving on those days, since the sight of Irv's opening his briefs—the "tighty whiteys," as Nathan called them—left them both in a state of shock, no matter how many times they'd seen it happen.

Still Chloe hoped that one day her mother would call her on the telephone and insist she come to the fabric store to see the newest lilac silk she'd gotten in that day. Together they'd run their hands over the yards of silk in their hands and lean together to examine the thread count.

"You could use a silk like this one for that doll you're planning," Chloe imagined her mother saying. "No one would look better in lilac than a Bingo Lady."

And Chloe would smile and press her face into the silk while her mother cut three yards of it for her with the shears she kept in her cotton smock.

She'd felt so much better sitting in the driver's seat with Harriet on her lap, but now, as she approached the house, the feeling of lightness began in her head again, a tingling sensation up and down her arms like the warning signs of a heart attack.

"I don't have anything to say," she told Nathan suddenly, stopping him at the front door, the smell of the Big E's manwiches wafting over them.

She knew that Nathan had long hoped that someday she'd come out of the shadows, that she'd shuck off the name Esther Bing and become her true self. Some small part of Chloe wished for that, too, she acknowledged, but not today, not with Irv and his kicking feet and the Big E piling ground beef onto bulky rolls while they waited for their next shifts.

"But I've got the perfect line for you," Nathan said, a look of pure dejection on his face. "You're the only one who can deliver it."

At her first doll show on the East Coast, she'd gone armed with a script Nathan had written for her. He'd diagrammed the booth where her Bingo Ladies were to be displayed and even projected questions the doll collectors might have about prices and proper care for the dolls. He'd even left room for haggling. When the collector named an agreed-upon price, he wanted Chloe to yell, "Bingo!" and raise the collector's hand in the air as if she were the winner. Chloe had sold several dolls at that show, but to Nathan's disappointment, had not once uttered the line.

As the Big E spooned heaping piles of sloppy joes onto their plates, Chloe couldn't help but notice the spark in her father's eye. He wiped at his tank top with his taped hands and eagerly watched as Nathan downed two of his manwiches and sloshed them back with a Spider-Man glass full of whiskey. Aunt Chickie gobbled down four, then begged to be excused, though Chloe knew she could have easily eaten a fifth if pressed.

"There's nothing like a good manwich to give you strength, right, Chloe?" the Big E asked. She forced herself to smile, letting the sauce drip from the sides of her mouth.

The Big E loved to feel he was of some use to the family, especially in his later years. When they were kids, Flo had been the main caretaker, driving them to the movies and carting Irv off to every comic book store on Long Island. Once she'd heard her father complain to Flo that if it weren't for her, neither Chloe nor Irv would even bother to ask how he was.

"It's not the old man they care about," he'd said to Flo on the porch one night while Chloe smoked cigarettes in the tomato garden. "You're the one they call."

She'd squashed the filter into the dirt with her heel when she heard him say this. Irv and her mother had started the tomato garden as a family project, though no one else had been allowed to water the plants or check for ripeness. She said a silent prayer that the plants would be overcome with bugs and singed a hole in one of the ripest ones before going back inside.

Now that Irv was a baby again, Chloe could sense that her father felt out of sorts, not knowing when to take his shift, ducking into the trophy room for curls whenever possible. He'd never changed diapers when they were infants, a fact her mother would boast about, conjuring up images of herself with diaper pins between her teeth and a baby on each hip. Since he hadn't helped on the first go-round, what could he possibly do now? He'd always made manwiches before every tournament, standing over the table and flexing his biceps while they murmured approval.

When everyone else cleared their plates and stacked them neatly in the dishwasher, her mother finally emerged from the basement. Her hair was tied in a knotty rag on the top of her head, her face streaming sweat. Nathan pulled a chair out for her and offered her a bun while the Big E slapped a pile of chunky beef on top, but her mother shook her head and waved the food away.

"Whose shift is it?" she asked, reaching for a Spider-Man glass and draining the last bit of whiskey. "Ruth's down there alone with him. Somebody else has got to go."

Not me, not me, Chloe thought, lighting a cigarette and blowing a thick cloud of smoke in her mother's direction. Her mother waved the smoke away with her hand. Chloe took a long drag and held it this time, turning her head to send the cloud in the opposite direction.

"If Ruth's down there, we don't need someone else right now, honey," Aunt Chickie said, laying a hand on her sister's shoulder. "Maybe some time alone would do them good. Maybe she can talk some sense into him."

Flo leaned forward in the chair with her head in her hands. Her arms were bruised on the sides, her hands cracked from all the diaper changing she must have done. Veins sunk in thick knots down her pale white neck, violet streaks that pooled in the V of her blouse.

"She could use the practice," Aunt Chickie said, reading a line that Nathan had slipped her under the table.

"Practice, huh?" Flo said, while Nathan whistled quietly to himself as if he'd had no part in the line. "You think she needs practice? She couldn't take care of him on her own."

Chloe swallowed hard and left her half-eaten manwich on her plate. The Big E sighed and dumped the pot of manwiches into the garbage pail, the thick brownish beef oozing out of the giant pot like thick slabs of glue.

"I can see where this is headed," the Big E said, not bothering to rinse the pot before depositing it in the dishwasher. "You'd rather do anything than talk about what the hell is wrong with that boy."

Chloe excused herself and made her way out the back door to what was left of the tomato garden. With her hands in the dirt, she dug a hole in the middle of one of the plants and buried what was left of the pack. She lit a match then and took several deep breaths, trying to clear her lungs. As she brought the match closer to the ground, she noticed a group of tiny white spiders scurrying out from beneath the mound of dirt. She dropped the match on top of them and watched as they ran to escape the flame.

Some time later her mother came and sat beside her on the ground. They said nothing for a while, just sitting with the earth under them and the sound of Irv's cries in the distance providing an odd kind of comfort. As she looked at her mother, she wondered how much her mother had forgotten. Didn't she remember all the afternoons Irv had snuck into the bathroom with a girlie magazine under his shirt? Didn't she remember the way he'd slurped at ice cubes noisily until Aunt Chickie had told him to stop?

When Irv entered adolescence, he'd put away his camera and spent long hours in the bathroom. No one had ever asked him why. He took to buying cans of Silly String and attaching them to his belt, spraying Aunt Chickie in the hallway when she went to the bathroom for her Desitin. Aunt Chickie had not found the practice amusing, and he'd only been prevailed upon to stop when she'd complained that the Silly String had wormed its way under her housedress and caused the chafing between her legs to burn even more hotly than before.

"Besides," Aunt Chickie whispered to Chloe one day, "it's unsightly for him to be shooting things from his belt. He's much too old for that."

Sometimes Chloe would catch Aunt Chickie looking at her mournfully as she got ready for school after Irv had slipped into Chloe's room at night. She wondered if Aunt Chickie knew, if she could sense the sickness bubbling up in Chloe's throat. Her mother had hidden the cans of Irv's Silly String in the cabinets and asked Chloe not to tell him after she'd found it in her search for sanitary napkins.

"Aunt Chickie doesn't like it when he sprays her," her mother said when Chloe asked why she'd hidden the cans. "He doesn't mean to hurt her, of course, but she doesn't like it."

One day Flo had come home from work and found Irv covered in a mass of Silly String. He'd found all of the cans and had spent hours spraying himself, his whole body matted and sticky beneath the mounds of string. She'd had to cut through it with scissors to free him. Afterward, there had been talk of sending for the priest who had married her parents, though Irv had promised he would stop. For a short time, they'd gone to church on Sundays, all of them in their Sunday best, the Big E choking in his tie.

Chloe picked at one of the tomato plants and offered her mother a cigarette. She'd been a smoker years ago, and occasionally, when she'd had too much wine at Christmas or complained of the stress of having to lug reams of fabric at the store, she would sneak a cigarette when the Big E wasn't looking.

Silently, her mother took the cigarette and puffed on it heavily as Chloe lit it for her. The tomatoes were wilting, the stems nearly broken, but she didn't seem to notice.

"We're going to need someone to look at him," her mother said. "Someone we can trust, who knows Ralph and who won't go dragging this to some newspaper like that poor homecoming queen, Darlene What's Her Name."

"Mulholland," Chloe said, surprised at how quickly the name came to her lips. "Darlene Mulholland."

Her mother coughed.

"Someone we can trust. Someone who knows what's best for my boy."

"What about that priest?" Chloe called.

Her mother turned in the doorway, the light from the living room spilling out across her face and leaving her shadow lingering on the lawn. Chloe stared at the shadow and watched it move as her mother turned in the doorway. If she would stay there, just for a minute, Chloe could think of what she wanted to say.

"What priest?" she asked, scratching at the rag tied on top of her head. "All we have is family."

As her mother headed back inside, she remembered the priest's name. Father Merritt. They would always count on a priest to help them, Chloe thought, bowing her head and staring at the burnt edges of spiders she'd lit with her match only hours before. She recalled the night she'd won the jackpot at the local church hall, how she'd been silly enough to think that Christ had brought her luck, that He had smiled down from the cross on the wall and had let her win the full card bingo.

"There's a bingo under the crucifix," the caller had said when Chloe announced her bingo, pointing to the wooden figure of Christ hanging over their heads.

All the way home they had said the line over and over again, howling at the way the caller had pointed at Chloe and then at Christ, the three of them laughing harder and harder every time they said the line until they no longer thought it was funny.

Homecoming Queen's Thorny Crown

(excerpted from *People* magazine)

The first thing you notice about seventeen-year-old Darlene Mulholland's bedroom are the teddy bears. They come in every color of the rainbow, all with one thing in common—they all wear the blue ribbon that has come to signify hope, justice, and the return of the 10 lb. 1 oz. baby boy known as "Bubba."

Mulholland sits in a large wicker chair with the blinds closed behind her to shield her from the cameras. Her mother, Wendy, a pretty forty-four-year-old with large blue eyes and a barrette tying back her graying hair, looks on nervously.

"I don't know how everyone started calling him 'Bubba,' Darlene Mulholland says, her voice shaky at first, then getting stronger as she gains confidence. "That was my private name for him. It was what I called him when nobody else in the world even knew he existed."

By all accounts, Darlene Mulholland was a normal teenager, having difficulty in Biology but maintaining a B average, Rollerblading with friends on weekends and dating some of the members of the football team. She was a well-liked babysitter and a trusted friend. Though she'd had several sexual partners, she'd never gotten pregnant and been forced to have an abortion, as several of her classmates had. She had been, according to friends, a lucky girl.

"It's scary that Darlene got pregnant," says Jessica Hine, class president. "There have been other girls who have gotten caught, but no one would have ever thought it about Darlene."

Even Mulholland herself seems baffled by her circumstances. She declined to answer why she didn't tell her parents of her pregnancy, nor will she reveal the identity of the baby's father. She does, however, offer some insight into the baby's disappearance.

"This has all been blown way out of proportion," she says, clutching one of the teddy bears sent to her from well-wishers around the country. "I mean, I didn't just dump him or anything. I went to get my crown."

Mulholland wipes her eyes with the back of her sleeve.

"I never even saw him," she whispers. "I don't even think I'd know him if I stepped over him."

When asked how she feels about her daughter's circumstances, mother Wendy says simply, "We know what Darlene did, and all we hope for now is that the boy will be returned to us."

Before the interview is curtailed by family attorney Lawrence Englebaum, Mulholland wishes to clarify a statement issued to the press.

"When I said aliens took my baby," she says firmly, "I didn't mean little green men. I meant men without green cards."

She coughs and looks hopefully at this reporter. "You know what I mean. Illegals."

Police have begun investigating custodial employees of Sagamore High, including one Hector Rodriguez, who emigrated to this country only three months ago. Detectives decline to comment on whether they believe Rodriguez may have been involved in the case, though they are examining his right to work in the U.S.

Chloe thought about the day that Gretchen died, curled up under her bed years after she'd moved out and Irv had gone on to become a clerk at the comic book store. He'd found the dog, in fact, while the Big E had searched the neighborhood in vain, whistling for her in his tank top.

Irv had been the one to call Chloe. He still lived at home at thirty and still watched Saturday morning cartoons in his underwear. Chloe had been working on one of the Bingo Lady's faces all afternoon, slicing the marbles for her eyes and sewing different shades of pale blonde mohair into her scalp. She soft-stitched one eye into a squint, tilted the doll's head to the right and left, but none of the expressions looked right. The doll's face eluded her like the remnants of a dream, coming into focus sharply for a minute and then fading again just as quickly.

"Gretchen died," Irv said immediately, his voice squeaking. "Under your bed."

He hadn't even bothered to say hello. She asked him how he'd found her, whether she'd been in pain, if they'd buried her yet. No, he said, and no again. He hadn't been able to drag her out from under the bed. Rigor mortis had set in, and no matter how many times he'd tried to slide her out, she'd resisted, her body swollen with death.

"Does Dad know yet?" she asked, picturing her father moving from door to door, sweating in his red tank top, the tape worn and unraveled on his hands, his flat-top wilting in the afternoon sun. She knew how much the Big E had loved the dog. He'd been so proud of the German Shepherd markings around her face and the way she'd been able to carry dumbbells around the house in her mouth when she was younger, dropping them at the Big E's feet at his command.

"No," Irv said, coughing. "I thought you could tell him."

The Bingo Lady's unfinished eye stared up at Chloe from the corner of her work table.

"Me?" she asked. "Where's Mom?"

This was one of the longest conversations she'd had with Irv in years.

"She took Aunt Chickie to the doctor," he said. "She's chafing again."

Later, on the drive to the house, Chloe thought about how many times she'd covered for Irv when he'd cut classes to hang around comic book stores and draw in his notebook, letting him steal her pennies at bingo, even sharing a jackpot with him when she'd felt badly that he almost never won.

She'd been too late to tell the Big E, who had found Gretchen after Irv had fled right after the phone call. He'd run from the house all the way to the comic book store where he'd later called from a pay phone and tearfully asked Flo to come and pick him up. The Big E stood in the backyard with Gretchen wrapped in a sheet, his hands a mass of splinters from the old shovel he'd used to dig her grave.

"She must have missed you," the Big E said. "I found her under your bed, croaked right there, dead as a doornail, the poor old broad."

As she watched her father dig the grave, she thought about Irv running from the house, leaving the dog under the bed with no one there to help her out from under, her hardened body covered with dust. She threw the old comforter on top of the dog's body as the Big E piled on mounds of dirt and then crossed himself. Even then, after so many years, the shadow of Gretchen's body and the needle-like hairs left an impression on the bedspread where she'd slept all those years, keeping watch.

When she finally reached the priest, Chloe told him only that there had been a family crisis, one that was not easily explained, and that her parents had asked her to call on their behalf.

"They're just too distraught about my brother," she lied, wondering if the priest could sense the deceit in her voice, the shakiness with which she'd managed to utter the word "brother." "They thought I should be the one to call."

She'd always wondered if priests had been blessed with a kind of clairvoyance, if they could read the thoughts of sinners. When she'd made her first confession, she'd lied to the priest, her knees perspiring inside the wooden booth. She'd told him that she'd taken cookies from her Aunt Chickie without permission and that she'd lied to her mother. Neither had been true. As a little girl, she and Irv had played games with pennies, making long tracks across the dining room table. They had scratched the finish of the table, a thought which had only occurred to her after the priest bestowed on her the penance of five Hail Marys and one Our Father.

The priest sighed heavily. She heard glass tinkling in the background and imagined him pouring sacramental wine into an opulent glass.

"Brothers and sisters need to care for each other," he said. "You're a good sister to call."

She gave him directions to the house and thanked him for his time. When she hung up, she found Nathan standing beside her scrawling notes on his index cards.

"I couldn't have said it better myself," he said, and then they held each other for a long time.

Before they went to bed, she left a note on the schedule for the others to read in the morning. In block letters she wrote: Father Merritt will arrive at 8 A.M.

Beneath the message, she signed her name in black ink. *Chloe.*

When she was thirteen, Chloe slept on the couch because she'd convinced herself there was safety in the living room. Irv had managed to navigate his way through the traps she'd set for him against her door, not disturbing the barbells and heavy books she'd left to cement the chair in place. After all the years of studying Spider-Man, Chloe wondered how much of the superhero's powers Irv had finally adapted. He seemed to move without detection, as if able to walk up and down the walls. He sensed the danger of being discovered and fled almost before she had a chance to open her eyes.

Her mother went to bed early, but Aunt Chickie often got up in the night to pat more Desitin on her chafed legs. Chloe could count on Aunt Chickie to stumble to the bathroom, for the sounds of her wincing to fill the silence in the room. The dog slept in a corner of the living room near the television, and though it was difficult to fall asleep with the sound blaring, Chloe was grateful that the Big E stayed up late watching reruns of old sitcoms, ever hopeful for a replay of one of his World's Strongest Man tournaments.

The springs in the couch poked through its thin foam, but Chloe welcomed them. With the springs digging into her back, she knew she would not sleep soundly, that she would be ready if Irv were to appear. She covered herself in heavy blankets and dreamed herself into a sweat, her face dripping when she awoke at night in the dark.

One night the television buzzed in the background, and the dog fell asleep with her tail curled under her chin. When the Big E had gotten up to go to the bathroom, she began flipping through the channels. He'd been in there for quite some time, having suffered a bout of indigestion after too many manwiches. She'd felt safe with the Big E so close by, with the dog in the corner on the carpet, the blankets pressing her into the couch.

On this night, a tournament was on. She thought of calling to the Big E to tell him, but from the sounds of the moans coming from the bathroom, she knew better than to disturb him. She tried to stay awake long enough to watch one of the Big E's rivals, Ken Patera, squatting against the back of a car for the dead-lift. She'd never liked the dead-lift event, not even as a kid, and had often hid behind her mother's pocketbook during this event, breathing in the leather while the crowd cheered.

She didn't remember what she'd been dreaming, but when she awoke, Irv's face loomed over hers. His eyes looked shockingly white with flecks of blue as his face moved away from hers, his feet sliding on the floor as he padded across the kitchen floor, down the hall to his bedroom. Her limbs felt leaden, sapped, as she lay there as quietly as she could, trying to sort out what had happened. She sat up and tried to breathe, looked over at the sleeping dog and behind her at the closed bathroom door. She heard the Big E groan. Ken Patera waved to the crowd, the muscles in his neck bulging.

With the back of her hand she wiped away the spittle left on her lips but did not allow herself to think about how it had gotten there, why his face had been so close. For a while she lay there and stared at the dog, watching her back rise and fall with the rhythm of her breath.

She lay there until her father emerged from the bathroom and sat in the recliner and closed her eyes, pretending to sleep. The tournament was over, the volume suddenly increasing as the scene switched to a car commercial. The Big E grunted and stifled a belch. She wondered if her mother had disappeared from her bed, if she'd floated away in the night and left her there with nothing but the television and the dog. Before she fell asleep again, long after the Big E had stripped the tape off his hands and shuffled off to bed, she tried to remember if Irv had been wearing a mask as he hovered above her, his white eyes glowing in the dark.

She and Nathan woke up to the sounds of bustling in the kitchen. Chloe held on to Nathan, startled, index cards spilling from beneath their pillows. Even pillow talk sometimes needed to be scripted, Nathan said. Sweet nothings were no less sweet if they'd been prepared.

"Jesus H. Christ!" the Big E shouted. "The goddamned priest is coming!"

Chloe pulled on a sweatshirt as Nathan gathered up his paper and Cross pen. The Big E stood in the hallway with a short-sleeved shirt and a striped yellow tie. She was shocked when she saw him; it had been years since he'd been persuaded to wear anything other than a tank top—not since Irv's wedding, she realized, and that had been no easy feat.

He must have seen the look on her face because he took her by the arm and led her toward the basement door.

"You did a good thing," he whispered. "Even your mother said so. She told me what a good sister you are, that you had the sense to call on the priest at a time like this."

Chloe nodded and fingered the raw spot on her hand where the glass had sliced through her skin.

"What can I do? I've got to do what that priest told me," he said. "I've got to cleave." He yanked at his tie and motioned toward the basement. "Now go downstairs and check on Ruth."

She just nodded and hurried down the stairs. This same priest, Father Merritt, had counseled them twice before—once when the Big E had strayed during the semifinals with a woman he'd met in a pool hall, and once when they couldn't get Irv out of the bathroom, just before the visits to Chloe's room had started. Her mother had always lauded the priest's effect on the Big E after his infidelity.

"Cleave to your wife, as the Bible says," the priest had told him, a sentiment the Big E would quote in times of trouble. Whether Father Merritt had told Irv he might go blind from spending too much time in the bathroom, however, Chloe had never found out.

The priest had not remembered her, though he seemed to recall the time Irv had locked himself in the bathroom and spoke of "the misfortunes of adolescence."

"Think of that poor girl from the papers," he'd said on the telephone. "We must learn to forgive. If there's anything left to do as a priest, it's to teach forgiveness."

She could hear Ruth moaning from the top of the stairs in a deep, sorrowful voice. For a moment she wondered if Ruth had slipped into labor while none of them were looking and that when she reached the back room she'd find Irv's new son lying beside him in a set of matching Onesies. But then she realized the whimpers were not from discomfort, but from a place much darker than physical pain.

"Ruth, honey," Chloe said, standing in the doorway so that she could see Ruth's body on the carpet but not Irv's head or his kicking baby feet. "Why don't you come back upstairs? I've sent for someone."

Chloe stood quietly in the door listening to the soft gurgling noises coming from the bassinet. She wondered what she might have done in Ruth's place, whether she would have lain there beside Nathan's shrunken body while her stomach grew even larger, the baby inside her twisting, anxious to burrow its way out.

Ruth struggled to a sitting position, her back arching as she heaved herself up.

"Who?" Ruth asked. "Not that homecoming queen, I hope. We have nothing in common. I have absolutely nothing to say to that girl."

It was clear Ruth was in a fragile state of mind. Why she thought the homecoming queen would be coming to their house, Chloe couldn't imagine. Of all the places Darlene Mulholland might go, why in the world would she come to save Irv?

"No, it's not the homecoming queen," Chloe said, then cleared her throat and spoke louder in order for Irv to be able to hear her. "It's a priest. Father Merritt. Ask Irv. He'd remember him."

Slowly Ruth shuffled to the doorway and leaned against it. Her hair was tattered, sticking out at the ends with bits of lint clinging to the sides, her large belly straining at a denim maternity blouse with missing buttons. When Ruth smiled, Chloe couldn't help but cover her mouth at the foulness of Ruth's breath.

"A priest," Ruth said softly. "That's good. Maybe he can save my boy." She lowered her eyes and held her belly with both hands. "I don't know how much longer my boy will last."

As they moved toward the stairs, Chloe felt Ruth's sticky fingers enclose hers, her body wilting to one side. Chloe considered asking her which boy she'd been talking about, which boy she'd meant to save.

Images of the priest throwing holy water at Irv's infant body while he vomited pea soup flashed through Chloe's mind on her way back upstairs. Her mother had told her the story of *The Exorcist* when she was eight or nine years old. She hadn't meant to scare Chloe, but the impact of the film had been so great that her mother simply had to share it with someone. For years Chloe imagined herself as Regan when she couldn't sleep at night, leaving the lights on to stop the demon from invading her, to keep her head from doing a 360-degree turn. She could not watch the film straight through without thinking of her mother coming in to check on Chloe after seeing the film with the Big E. Several times her mother had pulled up her nightgown at night to inspect Chloe's stomach for the words "Help me" gouged into her flesh.

Chloe held Ruth's arm as they climbed the stairs and maneuvered her toward the bathroom. She handed Ruth a pile of clean towels and a bottle of lavender-scented shampoo she'd bought on sale but had never used. As she stood and held the door open, Ruth turned to Chloe and squeezed her hand.

"Will you come in with me?" she whispered. "This bathroom gives me the creeps."

Chloe nodded and closed the door behind them. While Ruth undressed, Chloe turned her back and looked down at the cabinet where her mother had hidden the cans of Silly String. The water came on in a rush, and Chloe opened the cabinet slowly, murmuring to Ruth that she was indeed still there when Ruth called to her. She moved the jars of Desitin around, hoping to find a leftover can among the tubes of toothpaste and cans of air freshener. Although she was relieved to find that there were none, she couldn't help imagining herself standing over Irv's crib with Silly String in hand, spraying at his head and body until he was completely covered.

The priest was nearly three hours late, which gave them time, in Flo's words, to "sanctify the house." Her mother set out a cracked bust of Christ that Aunt Chickie had made during a ceramics class years before and dug out wilted palms from the attic. She Scotch-taped the palms to a plastic crucifix directly above Irv's head.

They draped a white blanket over Irv's bassinet that hung down the sides and spread over the bare floor. Chloe could see him from the doorway, the white blanket and crucifix forming a kind of mini-altar. Nathan set up folding chairs several feet from the bassinet in case they were called upon for audience participation.

He helped Ruth settle into a chair in the front row and handed her several of his index cards. He leaned down to sniff at her clean hair and smiled over at Chloe.

"An expectant mother can always use a good line," he told her, "especially when she has no idea what to expect."

Ruth shuffled through the index cards and sat staring up at the crucifix over Irv's head. The crucifix was crooked, Chloe realized, the plastic feet of Christ tilting out at an odd angle from the pale body yellowed with age.

"You think he'll serve the Eucharist?" Aunt Chickie whispered in the kitchen while Chloe finished setting finger sandwiches on a platter. "Maybe I should save my appetite. You're supposed to take the Lord on an empty stomach."

Chloe smiled and told Aunt Chickie she didn't think God would hold Chickie's appetite against her.

"It may just be me," Chloe said, "but I get the feeling that's just the kind of guy He is."

At her First Communion, Chloe had worn her hair in banana curls, having slept in foam rollers which left deep creases in her forehead where the plastic clasps had held them closed. On the line to receive, she'd stood next to a boy who called her "Curly" and whispered to her just before they climbed the steps to the waiting priest.

"My brother told me if you chew the wafer you go straight to hell," the boy said. "Whatever you do, don't let it touch your teeth."

"That's not true," Chloe had shot back. "My brother told me he chomped on his, and nothing happened to him."

The boy shrugged.

"Do what you want," he said, but later Chloe wondered whether it had been right to chew on a piece of God.

When the priest offered her the wafer, Chloe clasped her hands so tightly that she thought her knuckles would burst. She said her "Amen" with her tongue out, and walked back to her pew with the wafer stuck to the roof of her mouth as the Big E waved from his seat and gave her a thumbs-up. Her mother snapped a picture, and when the photo came out, Chloe's mouth was pulled to one side from trying to scrape the remnants of Christ from the roof of her mouth.

Flo waited outside at the edge of the driveway in a tan overcoat and a bandanna she'd made for the windy dead-lift tournaments on beaches where the Big E had won his World's Strongest Man titles. With a pair of Nathan's sunglasses hiding her face, she paced back and forth at the curb, reaching in her pocket for another of Chloe's cigarettes. She lit one after the other, a cloud of smoke enveloping her. Chloe watched from the window as her mother dragged on the cigarette, smoke dribbling from her mouth.

"Maybe someone should wait with her," Aunt Chickie said, but just then, the priest pulled up in a red cab and stepped out, standing for a moment at the curb with a black bag clutched in his left hand. They shook hands before Flo ushered him toward the door.

Aunt Chickie crushed a finger sandwich in her fist and said his name under her breath.

"Merritt, Merritt," she said, then threw the sandwich in the trash and smacked her lips together. "Father Merritt is here."

The Big E downed a last helping of cheese puffs and wiped his hands on his shirt, orange spots lingering on his tie and stiffly starched collar. Nathan and Chloe stood behind him, clutching each other's hands.

"*The Exorcist* scared the shit out of me," the Big E muttered, and then reached out to hold the door open for the priest, the seams of his shirt pulling at his biceps.

The priest smiled weakly and removed his hat, a black fedora, which Aunt Chickie took and set on a kitchen chair. He wore wire-rimmed glasses and a tight smile, his hair shaped in a gray crew cut which looked as if it had just been trimmed. Chloe was surprised at how much older he looked since he'd visited them during Irv's bathroom lock-up, the lines in his cheeks deeper, his once salt-and-pepper hair now completely white.

"Father Merritt," the Big E said, taking both of the priest's hands in his and pumping them up and down. "It's a hell of a nice thing for you to come. A hell of a nice thing."

Flo glared at the Big E as she removed the bandanna and sunglasses, the overcoat hanging uneasily about her shoulders.

"Yes, Father," she added, offering him a tray of finger sandwiches. "We can't thank you enough."

Merritt dismissed the tray and stepped forward to shake Chloe's hand.

"You must be the sister," he said. He shook her hand and thanked her for calling, then scratched at his crew cut and held a finger thoughtfully to his lips. "Your mother tells me you're a bingo player, too."

Chloe shook his warm hand and blushed. She glanced over at her mother, but Flo lowered her eyes and turned away.

"Of course the church doesn't officially endorse bingo," Father Merritt continued, stopping to wipe his glasses on his vestments. "Bingo winners are like people with stigmata. Happens all the time, and yet you never know which lucky one the Lord will choose next."

Flo moved ahead of them and took the priest by the arm, whispering to him before Nathan cut in.

"You mean the good Lord's a bingo caller?" Nathan asked.

The priest stood in the doorway clutching his black bag before descending the steps. They moved down in a processional, the Big E and her mother following directly behind the priest, Aunt Chickie trudging behind, Nathan holding Ruth's arm, and Chloe in the rear.

When they reached the bottom, the priest turned, not yet noticing Irv at the far end of the living room wrapped in white with a plastic crucifix above him.

"Personally, I do not sanction the church hosting bingo games," Father Merritt confided. "But we have to learn to choose our battles. There are a lot worse things in the world than bingo, after all."

"Amen!" the Big E boomed. He slapped the priest on the back and watched as Flo led him into the room.

The four of them sat in folding chairs—Chloe, Nathan, Aunt Chickie, and Ruth—as Flo and the Big E stood with their arms at their sides. The priest bent over Irv in his bassinet. He squinted and sniffed at the air as he assessed Irv's condition. Nathan shifted in his seat to remove a pack of index cards from his back pocket where he'd recorded his favorite lines from *The Exorcist*, just in case, he said, the priest didn't know them cold.

"The power of Christ compels you," he whispered, until Aunt Chickie shushed him and blew her nose.

"Have you ever seen anything like this, Father?" Flo asked, her voice trembling. "Do you think you can help us get my boy back?"

Ruth leaned forward, swaying as she hummed the Spider-Man theme song. Chloe wrapped one arm around Ruth's shoulders to quiet her, but the humming continued.

Father Merritt opened his bag and laid several items on the bassinet next to Irv. He slid his vestments over his head and made the sign of the cross over Irv's body. Irv squirmed and twisted his legs, his face squinched and red. A silver cross gleamed as Father Merritt held it in the air while Irv grunted, the color in his face deepening to scarlet.

The priest anointed his fingers with oil and traced his thumb over Irv's reddening face.

"In the name of the Father, and of the Son, and of the Holy Spirit," Father Merritt said. His hand trembled as he made the sign of the cross above Irv's body.

"In nomine patri, et filii, et spiritu sanctu," the Big E repeated. Flo leaned against him as he puffed his chest out with pride.

"All those years as an altar boy, Father," the Big E said in a stage whisper. "It never leaves you."

As Irv continued to twist on the bassinet, his grunting growing louder and more intense, the priest mumbled about the absolution of original sin and all children being welcomed into the Kingdom of Heaven. Flo reached forward as if to comfort Irv, but the priest held an arm up to block her.

"Do not listen," he said in a deep voice that rang through the room. "It is best not to listen."

Flo bit her lip and let her hands drop at the priest's command. Chloe felt Ruth rocking back and forth beside her as Irv began to groan, his knees twisting up toward his body, veins bulging at the temples.

"The Lord be with you," Merritt intoned, turning to signal to the rest of the group.

"And also with you," they answered.

"Let us pray," he said.

As they began the Lord's Prayer—"Our Father, who art in Heaven"—Chloe noticed that Irv's moans had subsided, the deep color in his face beginning to drain away. She squeezed Nathan's hand and waited for Irv's tiny body to levitate, for Father Merritt to reach inside his bag and throw an arsenal of holy water at Irv, who would writhe and snake his baby tongue in the air. As they reached the final verse, the smell was faint at first, but then became overpowering, the final "Amen" ending in an explosion of gas from Irv's diaper like a flurry of gunshots.

"Jesus Christ," the Big E yelled, reaching up to cover his face with both hands, "he took a shit!" They lifted their hands to their faces, Chloe pulling her shirt over her mouth and nose as the sickening smell permeated the room. Ruth gagged and shoved one of Aunt Chickie's tissues up her nose. Nathan buried his face in Chloe's shoulder. His Cross pen flew out of his hands and landed on the floor, and he scrambled to retrieve it.

Only Flo managed to breathe normally, reaching for a diaper as the priest began to choke. Father Merrit's knees buckled as he tried to move away from the bassinet, the vial of sacramental oil spilling over the carpet. He clutched at his chest as the Big E pulled him toward the kitchen, Nathan grabbing him by the other arm as Chloe threw open the window. The priest's face went white with shock, eyes rolled up in his head as he reached frantically for a bottle of pills and slipped one under his tongue. One hand still gripped the gleaming silver cross that he kept pressed to his chest. From the next room came the sounds of Irv's hiccups, high-pitched bubbles that punctuated the silence, echoing through the room like laughter.

Father Merritt revived in the kitchen after the Big E handed him a shot of whiskey. No one admonished Chloe when she offered him a cigarette. She watched the cigarette find its balance between his thumb and forefinger, the liver spots on his hand forming a lovely pattern of dots against his pale skin.

Finally the priest stubbed out his cigarette and stood up to leave. Aunt Chickie handed him his fedora, and Flo kissed his cheek to thank him for coming.

"Forgive my boy, Father," she said. "He knows not what he does."

Father Merritt nodded as the Big E held the door open for him and pressed a hand on the priest's arm.

"I want you to know I've cleaved, Father," the Big E said. "God knows I've cleaved."

The Big E asked Nathan and Chloe to help the priest out to the waiting taxi. As she passed him in the doorway, Chloe was startled to find the Big E's eyes welled with tears. She wanted to stop and offer some small gesture of comfort, to touch his taped fingers or kiss the cheek stained orange from too many cheese puffs. But the priest was eager to make his way out of the house, a feeling Chloe understood all too well.

At the curb Nathan eased Father Merritt into the back seat and handed him his black bag. His eyes were lined with pain, his cheeks and lips drooping.

"What do we do now, Father?" Nathan asked, holding the door for a moment and leaning in toward the priest. "I'm out of lines for something like this."

Father Merritt turned toward Chloe and stared into her eyes.

"There are demons all among us," the priest said softly. "Some of us understand that better than others."

He touched Chloe's cheek and whispered, "Pray." Then he reached for the door handle and pulled the door closed just as Nathan let go. They stood for a long time watching the taillights of the cab grow smaller in the distance, red spots of light that flickered at the street corner and then disappeared.

"Family Man" Cleared, New Questions Arise: Was Bubba Normal?

Associated Press

Long Island, NY:

Hector Rodriguez, a custodian at the now infamous Sagamore High School in Greenleaf Point, Long Island, told police through an interpreter that he had never seen the missing infant "Bubba," abandoned at birth by now-dethroned homecoming queen Darlene Mulholland.

Rodriguez had been detained by police following Mulholland's claims that illegal aliens "swiped" her baby.

"My client has six children of his own, four of whom are boys," said his attorney, Louis Gonzalez, an activist in the Hispanic community. "This is persecution, plain and simple."

Rodriguez claims that he noticed a pool of blood seeping from under one of the stalls in the ladies' room and immediately alerted his supervisor.

"He never saw any baby," Gonzalez maintained. "The fact that people are assuming a Hispanic man would steal a baby simply because of its whiteness is ludicrous. My client is a devout Catholic."

Meanwhile the search continues for the lost baby Bubba. Community residents have begun combing local beaches and parking lots, though authorities say that Bubba's chances of survival are now as low as twenty percent.

Neither police nor the Mulholland family could be reached for comment about the rumors that Bubba might have been born with some type of physical deformity. A tabloid journalist recently claimed to have obtained results of the study of Mulholland's placenta, which revealed the possibility of the infant's having an encephalitic head.

Encephalitis causes an extreme enlarging of the cranium, which some theorists maintain is the reason Mulholland abandoned the baby.

No such reports, however, have been confirmed.

Hector Rodriguez returned to his home after questioning. Onlookers say he was seen clutching his green card and crossing himself.

With the priest gone, Ruth took to sitting outside in the backyard and eating the half-ripened tomatoes that hung uneasily from the vines near the site where Gretchen was buried. The Big E stripped off his dress shirt and tie and headed immediately to the trophy room where he could be heard cursing as he power-lifted in his tank top.

"A boy needs a mother," Flo said while sucking on one of Chloe's last cigarettes. "And a mother has to be there for her boy, no matter what."

Nathan spent most of the day transcribing the priest's rites and vowing to say them into Irv's ear like a mantra.

"You'll see, Flo," he said. "He'll be wishing to God he'd never shit on that priest."

Chloe walked out to the garden and smiled down at Ruth, who looked up at her and continued eating the green tomatoes. They hadn't been sprayed or tended to in weeks, not since before Irv's transformation. She wondered if Ruth were purposely trying to make herself sick. Perhaps it might distract her to feel physically ill for a time. Irv had thirty-six years of babyishness in him. No newborn could compete with that.

Chloe sat beside Ruth in the dirt and lit her last cigarette. She looked out at the yard, at the patches of grass that had never grown back after Irv had built a huge spiderweb in the middle of the lawn. It had taken him weeks to fashion it out of branches, which he had wrapped in toilet paper and then spraypainted to whiten them and give them texture. While the neighborhood boys played street hockey and took girls to movie theaters, Irv obsessed over the giant web in the backyard. Her mother had praised his ingenuity and even had gone so far as to coax Irv into taking pictures of his web with his camera from his Peter Parker days.

"What does he plan to trap in that web?" Chloe asked her mother one day when her mother ran outside to cover it with a tarp to protect it from the rain.

Her mother had scolded Chloe for always criticizing Irv, for never trying to understand his imaginative powers.

"You think you know your brother but you don't," her mother said. "You have no idea who he really is."

Chloe had never disagreed. Sitting with Ruth among the tomatoes, she wondered if Ruth had ever known him, either, or if he'd simply settled into the void in her life and she had filled in the details. Perhaps she believed in the old adage that a man devoted to his mother would be equally devoted to his wife. Perhaps his boyish enthusiasm for Spidey had been attractive to her when she'd met him at the bingo hall. Perhaps the fact that he'd won the full card bingo that night had convinced her that Irv was a winner.

"He's not coming back, is he?" Ruth asked after a long silence. She smoothed her hair back with a dirty hand, smearing bits of tomato on the side of her face. "There's no way to get him back."

Chloe sighed. She knew that as a good sister-in-law she should say something to comfort Ruth, offer some bit of innocuous wisdom about bad things happening for a reason, about not giving up hope, about praying for a little luck to be thrown their way. She thought of how long ago, she'd been naive enough to believe that the fun of bingo was in the waiting.

But she said none of this to Ruth because she knew that Ruth liked bingo. After they'd married, bingo night had become a threesome, Irv and her mother in the front seat with Ruth in back along for the ride.

"It doesn't look good," Chloe said finally.

Ruth nodded and took a large bite of another tomato.

"What about Bubba?" Ruth asked in a whisper. "Do you think they'll find him?"

Chloe stubbed out her cigarette and rose to her feet, brushed off the dirt on the back of her pants. When she didn't answer, Ruth spat a piece of tomato on the ground.

"I think that homecoming queen should go to jail," Ruth said, holding the tomato in the air and staring at it. "Anyone who could leave her boy should be punished."

For a minute Chloe stared down at Ruth, at the chunks of tomato that lay scattered on the ground, the vines wilted by the shock of tomatoes being ripped away too soon. The homecoming queen's face loomed large in her mind nearly all the time, yet she found she didn't want to talk about her, not with Ruth. She looked behind her at the swell in the ground where the Big E had buried Gretchen, thought of her bones wrapped in the old comforter while Ruth sat with her legs splayed and dropped seeds all over the ground.

Gloria Rollins had opened the second NIADA convention Chloe attended with a song she'd chosen for the occasion. She was dressed as a huge rag doll with a magenta wig and flesh-colored mittens on her hands. An oversized straw hat sat awkwardly on top of the wig, cloth dolls with button eyes velcroed on every inch of her huge green-and-white muu-muu. She moved across the stage tossing dolls to the doll-makers who sat and shook their heads at the spectacle. She sang a bad version of the Beach Boy's "Rag Doll" and curtsied in her muu-muu.

"If there's one thing I've learned from being in the dolly world," she said before stepping down from the stage, "it's the importance of playing with yourself."

The room erupted in applause and laughter, as the dollmakers headed to their booths to set up their own creations. Chloe felt her face burn and tucked her rag doll under a pile of patterns she was selling that year at her booth. She found a large bingo card made of construction paper with her name written across the top, a present from Gloria.

"One of these days you'll have to tell me what it is about bingo that you love so much," Gloria said later that night when she came to Chloe's room with a bottle of wine and hunks of Gouda cheese. They sat cross-legged on the floor and sipped the wine from paper cups. "I could never see the fun in waiting for your number to be up."

Chloe laughed and downed a mouthful of wine.

"It's not that I love it," she said, feeling the wine bring a fine warmth to her cheeks. She glanced over the pile of index cards Nathan had written for her at the edge of her bed. "I guess it's a Catholic thing."

Gloria took a bite out of the Gouda cheese and smiled.

"I took Communion once even though I was raised a Lutheran," Gloria said. "I was married to number three then, and he had a thing about priests. The day he walked out the door, I said, 'You know, Larry,

I don't know what you believe in, but no self-respecting man would ever die for *your* sins.'"

They laughed and laughed, pounding the carpet with their feet. By the end of the night they were both so drunk, they sang the old children's "Bingo" song until their throats were sore and a dollmaker in pin curlers knocked on Chloe's door and asked them to keep it down.

"I don't know about you two," the woman said, pressing a hand to the curlers in her bangs, "but I have to get up early for my dolls."

When she was gone they clapped out the letters.

There was a farmer had a dog and Bingo was his name-o. Clap-clap-clap-clap-clap . . .

"It's a hell of a song," Gloria said, as they blew smoke rings at the ceiling and laughed. Before she left the convention, Chloe decided her next doll would be a woman in pin curlers who refused a jackpot out of principle.

Irv grew ravenous. Although Flo had sent the Big E for a case of Isomil and a package of diapers as soon as Irv had arrived, she was now down to her last can of formula. He sucked down bottle after bottle, Nathan keeping the helm at his head, supporting the neck and lecturing Irv about his responsibilities as a father as he swallowed the formula down in thick, choking gulps.

"My boy is starving, and I can't feed him fast enough," her mother wailed to the Big E, throwing her arms around his neck and staining his tank top with mascara. "I'm not mother enough for my boy."

The Big E patted her mother's back and peeled the tape from his fingers. Rarely had Chloe seen her parents engage in public displays of affection, though she remembered hearing their lovemaking whenever the Big E returned from another tournament. Her room was directly across from theirs, the hallway narrow between their doors.

A linen closet framed the end of the hall, where Irv would often stand pretending to look for bath towels, though Chloe knew that he was listening. As her mother moaned, he inevitably would lock himself in the bathroom, emerging only when the Big E pounded on the door.

As her parents embraced, Chloe watched Irv for signs of arousal. She believed he was sexless now, with his infant-sized penis, but how could anyone be sure? Even in that shell of a body, there must have been some part of the adult Irv left in him.

The Big E took over Nathan's spot at Irv's head and pawed at his temples. He'd never held them as babies, Flo had often bragged, because, in her words, no one was as capable as she had been. Now, thirty-six years later, the Big E looked like a new father fumbling with disposable diaper tabs.

"Hold still, Ralph, for crying out loud," the Big E said, as Irv's feet moved in the air, the large head twisting from side to side, his lips moving as he sucked and sucked. The Big E looked helplessly at Flo, who stood with Chickie against the wall. "Maybe there's something wrong with him."

Chloe couldn't help but laugh at this remark. Irv hiccuped loudly, a line of drool dangling from his lips.

"We know there's something wrong with him," Aunt Chickie said, getting up and smoothing the front of her rumpled housedress. "He's a baby, or hadn't you noticed?"

No one said anything for several minutes, even Nathan, who stepped back as if waiting for the Big E to suddenly erupt. People rarely challenged the Big E. Aunt Chickie had always spoken somewhat disparagingly of the Big E behind his back, whispering to Chloe about what a bad father he'd been to leave them at home while he was on the road for so long. In some ways, when she'd moved in, she'd felt as if she'd filled the Big E's shoes.

"I know he's a baby, Chick," he said through gritted teeth. "That's not what I'm talking about. I can see he's a baby, for Christ's sake."

Chloe stepped between them and pressed the upper part of Aunt Chickie's fleshy arm. This was her big chance—an excuse to leave the house.

"Nathan and I will go to the store," she said, turning away from Irv and looking straight at her mother. "There's hardly any food in the house now, and you need more formula. We'll go and get it."

She was breathless, pinching the flesh of her palm with her fingernails to try to calm herself, not to appear too excited. She grabbed a pen and yellow pad from the table and jotted a list as they called things out—Desitin, Wet Ones, larger nipples. A few jars of baby food might quell his hunger, her mother suggested, though her mother hoped it wouldn't spark an allergy.

"We've got to introduce rice at the very least," her mother said, coming to stand over Chloe as she wrote more and more items on the list. "This boy is starving."

Nathan hesitated for a moment, reaching for a fresh pack of index cards on the table, but Chloe grabbed his hand, hard, and pulled him toward the stairs. "Let's go, let's go," she said under her breath, feeling the tunneling in her mind as she glanced at Ruth through the backyard window, her hands and face covered in mud. Her feet pounded the carpet, the sound echoing through her body although she couldn't feel the ground.

At the supermarket they loaded the shopping cart with ten cases of Isomil, a huge package of Pampers, two giant-sized tubes of Desitin—one for Aunt Chickie and her constant chafing—and boxes of rice, cereal, and jars of baby food. Chloe purposely chose beets and carrots because Irv had always hated them. Revenge may have come in small doses, she thought as she placed the jars in the cart, but it came nevertheless.

Since there was little to eat but the Big E's leftover manwiches, they bought cold cuts and tuna fish, eggs, bread, chicken, and several different kinds of vegetables. Chloe chose some large ripened tomatoes still on the vine for Ruth in the hope that they might lure her out of the backyard. Surely eating unripe tomatoes could not have been good for her or the baby, though everyone seemed to have forgotten the real baby since Irv's transformation. Chloe hadn't forgotten him. She thought of his tiny hands instinctively reaching up to shield his ears from his father's screams. Chloe had read that unborn children could hear everything through the wall of the womb, and she fretted over the sounds that must have assaulted him in the liquid of his mother's cocoon. She wondered if he'd heard the priest's whispers and then the sputtering of gas that had ruined everything, as so much of his father's behavior already had.

In line at the checkout counter Chloe added several of the tabloids and three newspapers to the other items Nathan placed on the conveyor belt. She leafed through one of the tabloids as the checkout girl scanned the items and cracked her gum. A photo spread of the homecoming queen in her tulle dress fell out of the centerfold with arrows pointing to what appeared to be tiny blood stains under tremendous magnification. Other stills of her waving from the convertible taken from an onlooker's cam-corder covered a full page. The caption read "Heartless Homecoming Queen Waving as Bubba Languishes in Locker Room."

Chloe handed the tabloid to the checkout girl, who smiled at Nathan, her lip-gloss thick and shiny under the fluorescent lights.

"I see you two must have just had a baby," she said, giving Chloe a knowing smile. "How old is he?" She cracked her gum again. "Or is it a she?"

Chloe glared at Nathan as he counted out bills to pay for their order.

"It's a he," Nathan said in a deadpan voice. "And he's thirty-six."

He winced as Chloe stepped on his foot, the checkout girl's laughter ringing out over the whir of the cash register.

"Thirty-six?" the girl said. She ran her tongue over her lip-gloss. "You're a funny guy."

Chloe forced a smile.

"Thirty-six days," she said. "My husband's very precise."

The checkout girl laughed and gave Chloe the once-over before turning and stamping the cases of formula with "paid" stickers.

"Well, you'll get your figure back, don't you worry," she said, piling the jars of baby food into plastic bags. "I've got two boys of my own. It just takes time, that's all."

Chloe looked down at the shapeless T-shirt she was wearing but didn't respond. She moved ahead of Nathan and waited at the end of the aisle.

Later Ruth ate the tomatoes Chloe sliced for her at the kitchen table while Irv screamed between bottles. Every half hour Aunt Chickie emerged from the basement to reapply another coat of Desitin to her chafed skin while Flo and the Big E took turns pouring the Isomil down Irv's eager throat. Nathan sipped at his whiskey from a Spider-Man glass and smoked several of Chloe's cigarettes. He was always after her to quit, but with all that was going on, what point was there, he said. He lit one after another, passing one to Chloe and keeping one for himself. The priest's failure to return Irv to his former self had left him blocked. He fumbled with his pen and sighed heavily.

They helped Ruth to bed some time after midnight, where she stared up at the ceiling, a red ring crusted around her mouth. The room was a shrine to Irv with laminated comics lining the bookshelves and faded posters of the Green Goblin held together by pieces of Scotch tape yellowed with age. Chloe tucked the covers under Ruth's chin, her belly forcing the blankets upward and exposing her toes.

"The priest was right," Ruth said in a voice louder than Chloe had ever heard her use. Her hands smoothed the blanket covering her belly. "He should have cleaved."

Nathan nodded and made the sign of the cross over her in a sweeping gesture which Chloe found to be in bad taste, though it brought a smile to Ruth's lips. Within minutes she was asleep, her lips parted, air whistling through her teeth.

"You didn't have to go that far," Chloe whispered to him on the way to their bedroom.

"She thought that priest was going to bring her boy back," he said, as they readied themselves for bed. "Everybody needs something to see them through."

She thought of this as she hesitated to remove her blouse. Being naked in this room for more than several seconds always brought a dark blush down her neck, her chest covered with pink blotches. Nathan pulled her close on the bed before she had a chance to put on her thick nightgown, her breasts pressed to the springs in the squeaky mattress. No matter how desperately she wanted to feel that nightgown against her, she forced herself to lie there skin to skin until Nathan fell asleep.

As she lay listening to Nathan's snores later that night, she thought about the time Irv had locked himself in the bathroom. He'd been caught with several of the Big E's magazines, which he had thrown out the front window in the effort not to be found out. Chloe found them while hooking up the sprinkler one day, the glossy shots of pinkness startling her as she struggled to fit the nozzle to the pump. She didn't tell anyone about the magazines, but didn't twist the hose tightly enough, knowing that the Big E would have to come and secure it himself.

When he found the magazines tossed behind the bushes, the Big E screamed on the front lawn, calling for Chloe's mother and raging in his tank top. Later she was never quite sure if the Big E had been more upset by Irv's constant masturbation or by the defiling of his prized collection that nearly filled his side of her parents' walk-in closet. Chloe hid in the backyard with Gretchen while Irv barricaded himself in the bathroom, the priest arriving in a green station wagon and sitting by the door. She hadn't heard any of what the priest said, though she'd later dismantled the web in the backyard, cracking each branch over her knee and then throwing them in a pile. No one ever mentioned the web after that day, and for a long time afterward nights were quiet. By then she'd rigged a set of the Big E's barbells against the door and stopped hoping for a lock. And no matter how many times her mother asked her to join them, she never played bingo again.

Scientists Reveal Anomalies in Bubba's DNA

Associated Press

New York, NY

In a formal statement released this morning, Dr. Edward Gedrick, head of genetic studies at New York Hospital, revealed that a finding of genetic defects earlier reported by the tabloid newspaper *The Sun,* is correct.

Gedrick reported that a study of Darlene Mulholland's placenta did indeed show evidence of cranial anomalies.

Doctors have thus far been unable to specify exactly what type of genetic abnormality the infant may have suffered, though it is agreed that he would have had "a rather large head."

"The cranium would have been wider at the top of the skull and narrowed at certain facial points," Gedrick said.

Some analysts suggest that such a deformity might have caused Darlene Mulholland to believe she had delivered an alien, as she first suggested when she screamed, "Aliens took my baby!"

"The type of cranial shape this report describes is not unlike television depictions of alien life forms," said Susan Forth, a psychologist who counsels teenage mothers. "When she saw the head, she might have run in fear of alien abduction."

The Mulholland family, upon receiving the news of this report at their Long Island home following Darlene Mulholland's arraignment on charges of reckless endangerment and abandonment, issued the following statement read by their son, Josh:

"No matter what Darlene has done, we refuse to believe the idea that Bubba may have been deformed. This is yet another stunt by the press in order to make Darlene seem more heartless than she is. We await news of Bubba's safety every day and pray that whoever took him will return him to us."

As he turned to step inside the house again, Josh Mulholland allegedly whispered to a nearby reporter, "So he was a freak. A real live freak."

Mulholland family attorney, Lawrence Englebaum, denied that the homecoming queen's brother had ever made such a crude remark.

A sketch appeared in the tabloid depicting how Bubba might have looked. His head was large with two sets of webbed veins at his temples. The mouth, earlier pictured as bow-like, now appeared unnaturally small compared with the size of the skull. The bones near his temples protruded slightly above his ears, giving him the illusion of having gills.

"Christ Almighty," Nathan said, shaking his head. "No wonder that poor kid ran."

Chloe stared at the sketch until Bubba's features melded into a series of broken dots. She wondered how she could have been so shortsighted, how it had been possible to be so easily duped.

"Oh, my God, Nathan," she said. "What if this is Irv?"

He laid a hand on her thigh and squeezed. This was no time for hysterics, he said. Irv would have never had the wherewithal to pull off such a stunt.

"Besides," he added, "your mother knew it was him. Those teeth are a dead giveaway."

She nodded and took several breaths to calm herself, reaching in her bag to retrieve the pack of cigarettes. As she lit one and blew a cloud of smoke over the space in her headboard where her name had once been painted in swirls of lilac, she thought about the possibilities. The two teeth jutting from Irv's lower gums could not have belonged to anyone else. Irv's teeth had always been an eyesore, even after a brief stint with braces in childhood to correct a wayward incisor. His bottom teeth were jagged with large gaps between the front two, making him resemble an old man even in his early twenties.

She began to relax as she thought about the improbability that Irv might really be Bubba. Her mother loved to tell stories about the baby Ralph, before Chloe had come along, before he'd become Irv. Flo loved to boast that Ralph had known all the states' capitals by the time he was five and could read comic books at three-and-a-half. The Ralph her mother spoke of had been mature as a baby, with his precise diction and his preference for pickled herring over bologna sandwiches. In childhood portraits he'd always worn a bow tie and slicked his hair back at his own insistence.

"You're right," Chloe said finally, folding the newspaper sketch in two. "Whatever smarts Irv had went out the window after grammar school. He was never bright enough to make a clean break."

In the days since Irv's arrival, no one had even turned on the television, which was normally blasting in the living room with one of the Big E's programs on weightlifting or the infomercials he taped late at night advertising products to add bulk or workout equipment to increase the bicep several inches within days or your money back guaranteed. Chloe hadn't noticed the silence in the living room at first, but as she thought of the Big E's normal posture in his recliner, hunched over the television in his red tank top, she realized how much she missed his running commentaries.

"What the hell do these guys know about lifting?" he'd say. "Not one of them has ever won a refrigerator race or pulled a two-thousand-pound tram, that much I can tell you."

And then he would stand and flex both of his biceps, fists resting on either shoulder, squeezing so hard the veins threatened to burst through his skin.

Chloe hid the newspaper under the mattress while Nathan went to shower in the bathroom next door. She shifted the mattress back into position and sat smoking, thinking about the day her mother had thrown all of the Big E's magazines into the trash. The Big E had been away at a tournament in Florida, shortly after the incident with the priest. With Hefty bags her mother had attacked the closet, filling them with all of the raunchiest magazines, those with spread-eagled shots of matted pubic hair and exposed behinds. There was no airbrushing in the Big E's magazines, no gauzy lenses or soft come-hither looks. The Big E liked women the way he liked his weightlifting: hard-core and unadorned, full of sweat and veins, skin so puffed that the pulses seemed to throb.

She'd been late to school that morning. Her mother had let her oversleep and sent her to school with a note asking that Chloe be excused because of an upset stomach.

Dear Principal Boyd,

Please excuse Chloe's absence from homeroom and first period math class this morning. She is suffering from a bad case of diarrhea brought on by eating sloppy joes her father made from expired ground beef.

Sincerely,

Mrs. Florence Taft

When Chloe read the note, her face flushed with embarrassment.

"For God's sake, Ma," she cried, "couldn't you think of something else?"

Her mother dismissed Chloe's reaction with a wave of her hand. Mr. Boyd was a fan of the Big E's, having attended more than one refrigerator race over the years and even donating several old bus tires for tossing practice in the backyard. No one ever read those notes, anyway, her mother said. What difference did it make?

"Don't just stand there," her mother said, tearing the note from the pad and handing it to Chloe. Aunt Chickie was already toiling ahead of them, a Hefty bag thrown over one shoulder. "Help us get rid of these before the garbage men come."

It took two hands to lift the bag, the magazines bulging at the sides, the sharp corners threatening to stab through the plastic. She piled her bag on top of the others at the curb and hurried into the house again. Aunt Chickie closed the door and gripped Chloe's arm before her mother came back inside.

"Your father should have thrown these away a long time ago," Chickie whispered, "but who was I to say?" She wiped her face with a tissue plucked from beneath her bra strap. "You're not my kids, and this is not my house. I don't need to be told more than once."

Chloe slid her arms into the straps of her backpack. She waved good-bye to Aunt Chickie and moved down the driveway past her mother. When Chloe reached the corner of their block, she turned to look back at the pile of garbage bags at the curb. The garbage truck had stopped in front of the house, and the men were rummaging through the bags, their heads cocked as they pulled out centerfolds and turned them to the right and left, necks bent with their laughter. They threw several bags into the front seat rather than in the compartment where they were meant to be crushed.

The backpack pounded at her shoulder blades so hard it nearly knocked the wind out of her. Only when she could see the school in the distance did she force herself to walk slowly, stopping to take her mother's note out of her pocket and tear it into pieces that fluttered around her feet and scattered over the sidewalk.

Ruth stopped eating. She lay in bed with her arms folded and vowed not to let a single morsel pass her lips until either Irv returned or their son was born, whichever came first.

"Do you hear me, Ralph?" she screamed at the baby monitor on the bedside table, even though her end was a receiver, not a transmitter. "I'll starve to death! Two can play at this game!"

She slammed the monitor down on the table and clenched her fists. Chloe looked over at Nathan, who lifted Ruth's wrist and felt her pulse. The tomatoes had certainly enlivened her again, Chloe thought, as she tried to coax Ruth into eating slices of banana or a piece of toast. Maybe she'd brooded all night about the priest's words, Irv's failure to cleave. Even though she only went to church to play bingo, Ruth had been raised a strict Catholic. When Ruth's mother died several years before, Chloe remembered hearing that Ruth had gone to confession every day of the week for six months, though no one knew what sins she had committed.

Aunt Chickie made a western omelet and shoved a forkful between Ruth's lips, but Ruth spat it into her napkin and glared at all of them.

"Ruth, think of the baby," Aunt Chickie pleaded, wiping bits of egg from the sides of her mouth. "You're going to starve him."

Ruth smiled then, a slow smile that began at the corners of her lips and then spread to reveal her unbrushed teeth.

"He wants to be the only baby?" Ruth said, pulling the blankets up under her chin. "He just might get his wish."

Chloe couldn't stand to see Ruth this way, with her eyes red and swollen, her cheeks raw with burst capillaries beneath the skin. She'd felt sorry for Ruth for all of Irv's selfishness, but allowing her to starve their baby as retaliation was not something Chloe could condone.

"It's an act of desperation," Nathan said, as he closed the door behind them. "She knows that no matter what that priest said, Irv isn't coming back. And I think she's known it all along."

Aunt Chickie's eyes filled with tears.

"She's still got a baby to think about," she said, then blew her nose loudly. "She doesn't know how lucky she is."

Her parents joined them at the kitchen table. The Spider-Man glasses were dirty, and no one had bothered to run the dishwasher. They were reduced to drinking tap water from paper cups.

"Ruth's not eating," Chloe said, rubbing her eyes and reaching for a cigarette. She offered the pack to each of them, and they lit up one after the other, even the Big E and Aunt Chickie, who, as far as Chloe knew, had never smoked a cigarette in their lives. "She thinks Irv will come back if she threatens the baby."

Her mother flicked ashes into a paper cup and glared at Chloe. This was her mother, she thought, studying her face. This woman with a rag tied around her head who knew so much about silk. This woman with runny eyes, this woman who rarely smiled. "I really wish you'd stop calling him Irv," her mother said sharply. "I wish you'd stop saying that."

Chloe took a deep drag on her cigarette and let the smoke seep out her nostrils.

"Well, there are lots of things I wish," Chloe said. Her mother looked away and stubbed out her cigarette. She waited for a response, but her mother said nothing, just sat staring at the clock on the wall and rubbing her arms.

"Irv, Ralph, what the hell is the difference?" the Big E broke in. He took a long swig of whiskey that he'd poured for himself but had not offered the others. Nathan reached over to fill it as soon as he set the cup down again. "Call him whatever you goddamned please. He shit himself in front of a priest, for Christ's sake!"

There was no use condemning Irv's performance with the priest, Nathan said, since there had been no rehearsal, no subtext for motivation. The best thing to do now was to move forward.

"The show must go on," Nathan added cheerily, "even when the star flubs his lines—or shits himself, as the case may be."

The only way to draw Irv out of his infancy, Nathan suggested, was to find something that he'd want to come back to. Sad as it might seem, the impending birth of his son and his wife's wasting away were not things he'd mind missing. He had never really wanted the baby, anyway; even Ruth acknowledged that much.

"What does Irv love more than anything in the world?" Nathan asked. He held up a hand to silence the others. "Wait, let's hear from the Big E."

The Big E laughed and slammed his whiskey cup down on the table. "Spider-Man," he said. "That fucking Spider-Man."

Nathan beamed.

"That's right. And what does he love more than Spider-Man?"

The Big E downed the rest of his whiskey and stifled a belch.

"His goddamned birthday," he said. "Since the first time we stuck his feet in the cake, he's loved his birthday more than anyone I know."

Although Irv's actual birthdate was not for several months, why not push the clock forward a bit? Maybe all he needed was a reason to be reborn.

Aunt Chickie and Chloe nodded their agreement. The Big E pumped Nathan's hand and congratulated him on his efforts. Only Flo remained quiet, but in minutes, even she laid her hands on the table, palms upward, as if conceding defeat.

Nathan immediately assumed his party-planning mode. He began writing lists of favors and gifts, then pulled out his cell phone and ordered the best Spider-Man plates and crepe paper for decoration. Everyone would become Spider-Man for a day, except for the Big E, who agreed to take part on the condition that he be allowed to play the Green Goblin.

"At least the Green Goblin has some balls," the Big E said. "Spidey's a chickenshit web thrower, and that's all he'll ever be."

He left the table without another word.

With the party planning to distract them, Chloe began to feel a sense of dread at the thought of Irv's return. As long as he was an infant, she could almost pretend he didn't exist. In the basement he lived in the shadows, brewing with needs that could be contained in a bassinet.

To calm herself she slipped into her mother's bedroom to use the telephone to retrieve the messages on her answering machine. In her everyday life as a dollmaker, the phone was often her only real connection to the outside world, with orders from the fax machine pouring in or collectors leaving numbers with unfamiliar area codes after seeing her Bingo Ladies at doll shows. In the past year they'd had to install a separate line for Nathan's party planning due to the confusion of all the messages crowding the answering machine. When the telephone rang on Chloe's line, she could always be sure it was for her.

She sat on the bed with the princess phone on her lap and stared into the open walk-in closet across from her. She'd always found it amusing to imagine the Big E dialing the delicate buttons on the princess phone with his thick fingers, the receiver awkwardly poised in his other calloused paw. Since the Big E's official retirement from competition, her mother had made an effort to feminize the room with the addition of the phone and a flowery border above their bed, an eyelet cover with a matching frilly bedskirt. The closet on her mother's side was filled with pastel blazers and different colored flats which her mother wore only on special occasions. The Big E's side remained empty except for a few sport jackets and khaki pants which her mother kept in reserve for funerals and the occasional wedding. He kept all his tank tops in bureau drawers. Real men did not hang their shirts on hangers, he liked to say. The tie and shirt he'd worn for the priest's visit lay tangled on the floor at the foot of the bed. The shelves where the magazines had once piled up were now notoriously bare.

Her own voice came on after the third ring. She started at the sound of it, at the cheerfulness it conveyed, remembering how she'd read an article about the effect of smiling when answering the telephone. "Sound as if you've been waiting to hear from the person on the other end," the article said, and she had recorded her message afterward with a smile plastered on her face all the way through to the final beep. When she'd finished, her cheeks hurt from all the times it had taken to get the recording right, but the smiling had worked, Chloe realized as she listened to her voice on the tape. How odd it was to sound so eager to hear from herself.

The first two messages came from other dollmakers she'd gotten to know at various doll conventions over the years. Her friend Sarah called asking if Chloe knew where to get a particular type of mohair that had recently been discontinued, followed by a call from Gloria Rollins, who urged her to enter an upcoming show on Eastern Long Island. She said that with some lipstick and rouge and a cigarette hanging from her mouth, Chloe could become a Bingo Lady herself, and what better way to market her own dolls?

"Esther Bing is dying for panache," Gloria said with a sigh before hanging up, "but poor quiet Chloe just won't let her have some zing."

Several messages followed from women asking for patterns for Chloe's dolls, a practice she'd abandoned years ago. Collectors and crafters were fiercely loyal, a quality Chloe loved most about the doll world, and they often kept back issues of doll magazines for years, laminating their favorite interviews or clipping articles to be stacked away neatly in file cabinets. Once the Bingo Ladies had come to her, she'd stopped selling patterns. Gloria argued that patterning was a great way to make money, cheap and fast, but Chloe could no longer tolerate the thought of other hands sewing dolls she'd imagined, other fingers poking polyfill into bodies she'd designed. Now she made only one-of-a-kind dolls.

After the fourth message asking for patterns—had she and Nathan been gone that long?, she wondered, listening to the creaking sounds of the tape that signaled it was nearly full—she almost hung up.

"Hello," a woman's voice said suddenly, soft and rather hoarse, "I hope I have the right number. Someone named Gloria Rollins suggested I contact you about making a doll."

Chloe fumbled on the nightstand next to her mother's bed for a pencil and a scrap of paper. The woman cleared her throat.

"Dear God, where do I begin?" she asked, then let out a long sigh.

Chloe held her pencil and waited. She wondered who Gloria might have sent to her. Chloe rarely fulfilled requests not related in some way to her Bingo Ladies. Gloria traveled almost constantly, giving seminars on the merits of doll interaction to everyone from recovering addicts to Wall Street brokers. This woman could have been anyone.

"Gloria assured me you were a trustworthy person," the woman said, "although I don't believe that about anyone anymore, not after all we've been through."

She sounded as if she were going to hang up, when her voice came on again in a rush.

"My name is Wendy Mulholland. The homecoming queen is my daughter. The one from Sagamore High. The one from all the papers. The one who delivered our Bubba."

Chloe dropped the pencil on the floor.

"I'm calling because . . . well, because . . . because there's nearly no chance that we'll ever get Bubba back, at least that's what the police say, he's either starved by now or worse, and I want you to make a doll for us. A doll that will help us remember him. If you think you can do that, call me at this number."

She said the number so quickly that Chloe nearly missed it, having to reassure herself the woman had said "three" and not "five" because she didn't think she could sit through the list of messages again. She scribbled the number down as quickly as she could and sat with the receiver pressed up against her chest.

Maybe she should find Nathan before making the call, she thought, have him write her a script complete with pauses and multiple choice options. Even though she wasn't sure what she would say, she realized that making the call on her own was something she had to do.

The person on the other end picked up the phone but said nothing. Chloe could hear the person breathing, slowly and patiently, waiting for her to speak. They probably got calls from reporters constantly, though she couldn't think how to begin without having the phone slammed down in her ear.

"Hello?" she said finally. "Is this the Mulholland home?"

Heavy breath pushed static through the receiver.

"I received a call from Wendy Mulholland," she continued. "The homecoming queen's mother."

She knew it was a stupid thing to say and blushed though there was no one in the room. Before she continued, she lit a cigarette and took a deep drag.

"This is Esther Bing," she said, certain that it was Josh Mulholland on the other end, the outspoken brother who had been seen outside the family home looking up in the sky as if for aliens. "Tell your mother Esther Bing is on the phone."

She heard the receiver drop with a thud, though the connection wasn't broken. Muffled voices echoed in the distance, the sounds of the harried goings-on of a family in crisis. Chloe knew those sounds all too well. She took long drags on her cigarette and waited.

The receiver crashed before the mother's voice came over the line.

"Esther Bing?" the voice asked, as if on the verge of tears. "Is it really you?"

Chloe swallowed several times before answering.

"Yes," she said softly. "It's me."

She twisted the cord between her fingers and held her breath.

"I've seen some of your bingo dolls," Mrs. Mulholland said, "when

I met Gloria at a doll show a while back, before I knew Darlene was pregnant, before any of this happened . . ."

Chloe nodded, though she realized the woman couldn't see her through the phone.

"I used to take the kids to bingo all the time when they were younger," she said. "Darlene never liked it all that much, but Josh, he was a fine bingo player, you know? One of the finest I've ever seen."

Chloe had never heard anyone described as being a "fine bingo player" before, especially since the game required no skill, unless you counted a halfway decent attention span. She imagined Josh in his tight denim jacket, his shoulders hunched over a bingo card. Darlene going over her card with a bright pink blotter.

"You must have enjoyed bingo yourself," Wendy Mulholland said. "It must have a special place in your heart, with all those dolls you've made."

For a minute Chloe considered what Mrs. Mulholland might have said if she told the truth, that life had changed more than anyone could have guessed after bingo, that her dolls were spirit catchers, not tributes.

"Actually, I hate bingo," Chloe blurted, exhaling smoke. "But that's not what you want to talk about. You want to talk about Bubba."

She wondered if Darlene were nearby, if the girl were sitting in her room strewn with teddy bears rocking back and forth on her canopy bed with a broken crown on her head. *You shouldn't have run,* Chloe wanted to tell her. *Running got you nowhere.*

"Yes, Bubba," Mrs. Mulholland said finally. "I know you usually make women, but I was wondering if just this once you'd make a baby for us. A baby Bubba, one who won't get lost."

Chloe asked some preliminary questions: when did the family want the doll, and how could it be kept from the press? She spoke briefly about how she worked and said that she would try to deliver the doll within a week—an extraordinarily small amount of time, but she was willing to make exceptions in this case. They would work out details about the location for the drop-off when the time came, they agreed.

"Thank you, Esther," Mrs. Mulholland said just before the connection was broken. "This means so much to us. We can't tell you how much we want that boy back. He's our little cherub."

The phone went dead before Chloe had a chance to reply. She wanted to ask why they only missed Bubba now that he was gone, and more importantly, how they could miss someone they'd never known or even seen. How could they have lived in a house with a daughter whose belly had expanded with every passing day without ever noticing how much she'd changed?

As she closed the door to her mother's bedroom and walked back toward the kitchen, Chloe thought about how she would manage to get home to gather materials without being missed. No excuse would be good enough to leave, even though they'd been there nearly a week and had said nothing about when they might be going. Her parents knew Nathan had no upcoming plans besides a corporate retirement party with a Broadway theme at the end of the month. She kept a part-time job mending wedding gowns for a seamstress as far as her parents knew, a job she'd fabricated several years ago to keep them from thinking she did little else but smoke and watch bad television during the day, wasting her education. She needed a reason to discuss fabric, though she wouldn't reveal the truth about her dolls.

She found her mother sitting alone at the kitchen table as she got ready to leave. Nathan had gone back to the basement to read the few words the priest had spoken. For improvisation, he'd brought Aunt Chickie down with him, her mother told her, to recite the Apostle's

Creed. Even the Big E had been enlisted to intone the few Latin phrases he remembered from his days as an altar boy when all of the masses had been in Latin, though he needed to get drunk in order to do it.

"I gave him plenty of whiskey," Nathan had said. "Without it, he gets stuck on the 'Domine, Domine,' and that's as far as it goes."

Chloe sat down beside her mother and smiled at the memory. The Big E rarely drank in his days as a power lifter, not because he objected to drinking but because bad hangovers sapped his strength. After every win, however, he'd invariably sit with his whiskey bottle and croon the Latin masses on the edge of his bed.

"Dominus vobiscum," the Big E would drunkenly belt, his hands over his heart, tank top rumpled, "Et cum spiritu tuo."

He'd suspend the "tu" in "tuo" until he fell back on the bed and applauded himself.

"All those years of Catholic school," he'd say. "The goddamned crap gets into your guts."

Chloe passed her mother a cigarette, but she refused it, standing and moving to the kitchen window. The small of her back curved, and she seemed to become smaller, her neck and shoulders slumping forward.

"Mom," Chloe said. When she didn't respond, Chloe spoke again. "Mom."

Her mother turned, and for a moment, Chloe imagined she were the homecoming queen pregnant at the kitchen table, her mother staring right through her—past the bulk of sweatshirts that had hidden Bubba, past the dreams of tulle and a glittering crown. In that moment, she imagined her mother saw the girl alone in the stall, bare feet on cold tile, blood soaking armfuls of white towels. The girl alone in her bedroom with only the darkness to protect her.

"What is it?" her mother asked.

She looked at her mother standing there with the light from the window at her back, her head cocked toward the basement, waiting for the sounds of Irv's needs. She watched her mother looking past her, and said nothing.

Homecoming Queen Shocker: Brother Made Her Do It

Associated Press

Greenleaf Point, NY

An unnamed source close to Mulholland family attorney Lawrence Englebaum issued a shocking statement regarding Darlene Mulholland's motive for abandoning the infant known as Bubba fourteen days ago.

"The truth will show that Darlene admits to being traumatized at the time of the infant's birth, which led to painful childhood flashbacks of her older brother Josh's fascination with physical deformities," the source said.

The source referred to a copy of the famous book *Freaks* as specific evidence for Darlene's fears. According to the source, the homecoming queen stumbled upon her brother's collection of books and videos at a most vulnerable time in her life.

"She was apparently terrified of a man with an enormous head and a tiny body who was known as 'The Caterpillar Man.' When she saw the infant emerging from between her legs, she immediately went into shock and, according to a psychologist specializing in the field of childhood trauma, actually thought that the infant was indeed the Caterpillar Man when she abandoned him," the source said.

"Therefore," the source asked, "how can she be held responsible for abandoning a baby she didn't really recognize as her own?"

The statement came on the heels of District Attorney Madreski's prediction that Englebaum would try to plea bargain to avoid a prison term for his client.

Friends of Josh Mulholland recall a youngster prone to practical jokes who believed physical disfigurement and alien life were directly related. Josh frequently drew pictures of his sister with a gigantic head and bulging eyes to show her what she might look like as an alien life form.

"He did have a thing about freaks," a friend, who requested anonymity, said this afternoon, "but not in a bad way. He thought they were cool, like not of this earth or something."

Another friend cited Josh's fascination with the film *The Elephant Man,* which he often watched as much as three times a week. The film, starring renowned British actor John Hurt, depicts the life of Joseph Merrick, a man sold to a sideshow and persecuted horribly for his deformities.

"He thought [the Elephant Man] had a really cool head," said the friend, who also asked to remain anonymous. "He wondered what it would feel like to have a head that huge."

The Mulholland family is expected at the County Superior Court tomorrow afternoon where Darlene Mulholland will face a grand jury. It is unknown at press time whether Josh Mulholland, the outspoken brother of the homecoming queen, will appear with the family.

Chloe and the Big E sat side by side on an old picnic bench next to the marker on Gretchen's grave. The earth still expanded there ever so slightly as if Gretchen had never been able to rest easily, even after all these years. Irv had that effect on animals; he was unsettling. As a housewarming present, Flo had given Ruth and Irv a kitten named Boots, a kind of practice baby with gray stripes and white paws. The kitten, which must have been weaned from its mother too soon, loved to suck on old wool socks when Boots and Ruth were alone in the evenings while Irv worked at the comic book store. When Irv got home, the cat would run up the drapes and claw the rug in a frenzy until eventually they had to return it to the shelter.

"The woman there said Boots had separation anxiety, and that's why she acted so crazy," Ruth had said tearfully on the phone when she'd called Chloe to tell her what had happened, "but I think she was jealous of Ralph. When she was with me, she was the sweetest thing, but once he got home, she'd go berserk."

Chloe sat quietly as the Big E picked at the tape on his fingers. Ruth still lay in bed where she refused all of the goodies Aunt Chickie tried to tempt her with: Fig Newtons, Ring Dings, even Flo's favorite during her own pregnancies—macaroni and cheese with bits of hot dog stirred in then baked with sprinkled paprika. Aunt Chickie had spent the better part of the day not only trying to come up with the perfect concoction that would spark Ruth's hunger, but had even raided her own private stash of junk food which she kept hidden in a hope chest in her bedroom closet.

Finally Aunt Chickie came outside in her housedress, her lipstick smeared, and stood wiping her sopped face with the neverending supply of tissues trapped beneath her bra strap.

"She just won't eat, no matter what I do," she said.

The Big E stood and offered Aunt Chickie his place on the picnic bench.

"Ah, Chick, if you were a parent you'd understand," the Big E said with a sigh. "You bring them into the world and they do whatever the hell they want, no matter what you do to try to stop them, especially the boys."

He winked at Chloe.

"I suppose you're right," Aunt Chickie said, and then they were quiet for a long time, the three of them listening to Irv's muffled cries.

Chloe sat thinking about how she might make her getaway. Nathan had gone out on a party run to buy streamers and Spider-Man masks. She struggled to think of something he might have forgotten, something she might have to get in order to give the party its finishing touches. If her motives seemed to concern Irv specifically, she knew no one would question her.

She was about to go into the house for another pack of cigarettes when her mother appeared in the doorway. At first Chloe couldn't tell why her mother was crying, though she could see from the look on her face that something had gone wrong. The three of them moved toward her, the Big E leading the way.

When she stepped outside, Chloe had to cover her mouth to stifle the smell. The vomit was everywhere, thick and white, in her mother's hair and eyes, down the front of her pale blue blouse.

"He got sick all over me," her mother said, wiping her face with one of Aunt Chickie's tissues. "Maybe Father Merritt got to him more than we thought."

The Big E took off his tank top and held it out like an offering. Barechested, he stood there helplessly as she took it, smearing the sticky formula over her face and hands.

"Maybe we pushed him too hard," her mother said, her voice choking.

"I don't know what else I can do for him. What else is a mother supposed to do for her boy?"

She collapsed on the bench and held her face in her hands. The Big E kneeled in the dirt and wrapped his arms awkwardly around her, the red tank top making a low squishing sound as the formula seeped between them. Chloe stood watching her father with his arms stretched around her mother's shaking body, their arms and hands flecked with spit-up.

Without looking back at them she stormed down the steps to the basement and headed straight for the bassinet. She didn't hesitate this time, not even at the sight of his giant head, the small pathetic feet kicking from beneath his swaddling blankets. His bottom lip dripped blobs of formula down his chin that pooled in the skin above his undershirt, the skin of his neck stretched thin with veins and pulsing tendons. It would be so easy to snap that neck, she thought. All she'd have to do was lift his head and then let it fall.

As if he could sense what she was thinking, Irv's lower lip began to tremble, the two adult teeth jutting from his gums. He turned his filmy eyes toward her, blinked furiously, and then stared.

She thought of all the things she could say to hurt him now that they were alone, all the rage she could finally release, all the years of pretending she didn't know what he'd done. She could tell him she knew it was his eyes staring at her in the darkness of her bedroom, not the dog's, that it was his breath she still heard on sleepless nights, slow and muffled as if through a mask.

Instead she said the one thing that she knew would torment him more than anything else.

"Hey, Irv," she whispered, leaning down so close that the force of her breath caused his eyelids to flutter. "Spidey would be ashamed of someone like you."

She paused and collected herself.

"What the hell did you ever know about Spidey?" she said, then pulled the blanket away from his head so that every vein showed, every imperfection. "Spidey cared about people. He didn't hurt them. You couldn't be Spidey if your life depended on it."

She turned her back on him and started to walk away, waiting for the sounds of his screams to fill the close air of the dank basement room. Before she reached the stairs she turned to look at him one last time. From across the room she could see the tears welling up and then falling slowly.

When Nathan came back, Chloe pulled him into the bedroom and closed the door. There wasn't time to explain, she said, but she had to go home. She had a doll inside her that needed to be made. Nathan asked her if the doll could wait, since Irv was on the cusp of rebirth, and if she left now, she risked missing the party.

"I'm even going to stage a fight with the Big E as the Green Goblin and Ruth as the damsel in distress," Nathan said, reaching inside the party bag to show her the favors he'd bought—Pez dispensers with Spider-Man heads, even a glow-in-the-dark Jell-O mold in the shape of the Green Goblin's face.

Chloe smiled weakly and fingered the red noisemakers and streamers spilling out of the bag.

"I'm doing this for you," Nathan said softly, tickling the back of her neck with his fingertips. "We'll have tried everything we could think of. Nobody could ever say any different."

She faced the wall beside her bed where she had been awakened so many times. She thought about the nights spent waiting for the sounds of her brother's breath growing faster in the darkness. Everything had changed for her on those nights. The world she lived in had grown darker somehow, the ground under her feet less stable. She'd walked around for weeks trying to balance herself, as if someone might suddenly come along and pull the floor out from under her.

"I've got to go home," she said, as firmly as she could manage. "Someone needs me to make a doll."

She headed outside to the car and fought to open the door despite the shaking of her hands, the feeling that her body was no longer her own. She strapped herself into the driver's seat as Nathan banged on the window, pausing only to open it a crack.

"Can't you tell me who the doll's for?" Nathan asked, his voice hoarse. "Chloe, please."

She slipped the gear shift into drive and released her foot from the brake, letting the car roll forward a bit as Nathan ran along with her.

"I'm sorry," she said. She didn't know why she couldn't tell him who the doll was meant for; she knew he'd have kept the secret. All she had to say was, "It's for the homecoming queen," and he would have immediately understood, but she couldn't force the words out of her mouth.

She could hardly stop long enough to dislodge the keys from the ignition. Bursts of nicotine pulsed in her veins, and she ran up the steps to the front door two at a time, flinging the door open and stepping over a week's pile of mail. Normally she would have examined each piece, anxious to hear from collectors and the agent who had contacted her about a studio show the following spring.

She went straight to her work room and turned on all the lights, standing for a brief moment and letting the smell of glue and fabric fill her lungs, the high odor of nylon suffusing the room. All of her fabrics and needles lay in their crates and trays waiting for her. With a rush of energy she lit a cigarette, dumped the contents of the boxes all over her table, and clipped the police sketch of Bubba on the clothesline she kept strung across the room.

As she pressed her charcoal pencil to paper, she imagined Darlene and her mother sitting in a white wicker room, waiting for the Bubba doll to fill the empty crib. She sketched him in different poses, lying in a bassinet with a mobile of multicolored teddy bears spinning above him, on his changing table with his lips puckered as the homecoming queen slathered his bottom with ointment, his mouth open in a yawn. She sketched and sketched, forcing herself to repeat Mrs. Mulholland's words in her head over and over.

"We want to remember him as he might have been," she'd said, her voice strangled by tears. "He's our little cherub."

When Chloe finished drawing she clipped each sketch to the clothesline and stared at them, waiting for the sudden flurry of excitement that happened inside her just before she began with the first twists of the armature. Without this flutter she could never begin. She had to believe that somehow she would suffer if a doll were not created. There was no telling when this feeling would appear. Sometimes she waited for days or even weeks to feel it, but with this doll, she didn't have time.

She walked from one end of the clothesline to the other, lingering at each sketch and sucking in smoke. Twice she stubbed out her cigarette and sat down to begin despite the feeling's refusal to appear. Perhaps Bubba was simply a doll she could not find it inside of her to make. She would have to call Mrs. Mulholland and break the news to her.

"Please forgive me," she would say, "but he looks too much like my brother Irv."

As soon as she imagined the conversation her stomach quivered, a twisting that began under her navel and spread down and across her abdomen. How could she have been so stupid, she thought, as she began shaping the wire armature, leaving a thick ball where the head would be and twisting the spot where the neck elongated from the base of the enormous skull. This Bubba would be real, with blood caked in his ears and only white towels for blankets. She would invent him the way she imagined he had been in those first moments of life—not cuddly and perfect, as Mrs. Mulholland might have thought he had been—but purple and frightened, the tendons in his neck stretched taut with the strain of holding up his oversized head. She would use balls of cotton for the bubble of fluid that rested over his right eye, long strips of blue yarn for the veins that had surely wriggled beneath the thin sheath of skin covering his skull.

She began with the head, as it was the most difficult. With other dolls she often started with the overall structure, padding arms and chests, middle sections and legs that gave way to finely detailed feet. On the work table she kept a diagram of a human skull and a rubber foot from a party store that Nathan had bought her when they'd just married to give her a model to work from, to perfect the arches and tendons, the lines through the ball and down along the heel. As she sculpted the first bits of the nylon head with her needle, she wished she had a copy of the book on deformities Josh stashed in his room. She might have found inspiration in The Caterpillar Man, though she highly doubted Bubba had ever looked that way.

By four o'clock in the morning she'd formed the entire body and skull, and begun to work on the hands and feet, which she imagined to have been violet and pasty, like the newborns she'd seen in books on giving birth. Occasionally she studied these books to understand new life, sneaking them into her work room and poring over every detail. She found one of the books under an old box of mohair she'd used for a Bingo Lady from the life-size show she'd done several years ago in Chicago. At a garage sale she'd found a long rectangular table where each of the Bingo Ladies sat, anxious hands poised to mark off the numbers that had been called. She'd sold the entire exhibit for nearly thirty thousand dollars to a wealthy collector from the North Shore who had never played a game of bingo in her life.

As she leafed through the birth book, she settled on the centerfold, a full color photo of an infant with the yellow umbilical cord running down from its belly and between its legs, its face contorted with exertion and pain. There was something so cruel about birth, she had thought as she'd studied these books then, a profound struggle to be free.

She fell asleep at the work table as she tried to decide on the right materials for Bubba's eyes. She dreamed that she and Irv were playing bingo in the high school gymnasium at a long cafeteria table, the kind with benches attached. At first she thought that she and Irv were part of a live exhibit, with the multicolored chips fastened to styrofoam cards with a hot glue gun.

"Are we real, or are we dolls?" she asked Irv.

He shrugged and covered his bingo card with both hands.

"No peeking," he said.

Their mother moved toward them, steam rising from the plate of hot bagels she was carrying.

"Kids," their mother called, "don't you want something to eat? You can't play bingo on an empty stomach."

Her mother stuffed a bagel into her mouth and suddenly began to grow larger, her body expanding until she reached the size of Aunt Chickie. Irv clapped and stood up from the bench, tearing his card from the table and holding it high in the air.

"Bingo!" he yelled over and over again, waving his card at the bingo checkers who paced up and down the aisles without ever glancing in his direction.

"Can't you see I'm the winner?" he screamed. The sockets of his eyes turned white.

She threw his card to the floor and stomped on it over and over again, styrofoam crackling beneath her feet.

"You always win," she said, as their mother came toward her, hiking her housedress higher with every step. "I'm so sick of you winning."

Chloe kicked the bits of styrofoam under the table and ran toward the door. As she reached the end of the hall, she turned and saw her mother with her house dress pulled up above her waist, revealing a pair of red Spider-Man panties.

"Help me close my eyes," Chloe whispered to the man calling out bingo numbers in a gravelly voice. "I need to close my eyes."

But the bingo caller handed her a daisy instead, his webbed hand clinging to hers.

"It's too late for that," he said. "That's how it is with bingo. You've got to see to be able to play."

She dropped the daisy on the floor and ran out to the parking lot where Gretchen lay dead on the asphalt. When she leaned down to listen for the dog's heartbeat, she heard a baby crying in the distance. Women with painted faces rushed toward the dead dog, but no one bothered to try to find the baby.

When Chloe awoke she immediately began sculpting Bubba's eyes closed. His face was twisted in an expression of anguish, as if he had seen too much even in the few moments he'd been alive. If he were going to be left alone and unprotected, the least she could do was to seal his eyes against the pain of being witness to his own abandonment.

Though she'd slept little more than an hour or two, she felt remarkably energized. She stood up from the table and set Bubba on an old white towel she'd found in her linen closet. She sewed the edges of the towel behind his shoulder blades and at his ankles, cross stitches that allowed the towel to sag between his legs. She'd set him in the act of squirming, his fingers clenched, the large head turned slightly to the right, feet at a slight angle in the air. The towel hanging from his feet gave him the illusion of movement. She could almost see him struggling to either break free of the towel or burrow himself more deeply. She was sure others would see him fighting to find warmth, but she preferred to think of him in the act of escape, not simply lying in wait while his mother ran off in her white tulle dress to gather her crown.

In a last moment of mercy, she removed the well of fluid above his right eye. Then, as she smoothed the space beneath his eye where the lump had been, softly gathering the nylon into a delicate patch of untouched skin, the telephone rang. At first she thought of not answering it, but she knew Nathan would be worried if she didn't.

Since she knew it was her line and therefore only for her, she didn't bother to say hello, just held the receiver to her ear and lit a cigarette, exhaling a thick cloud of smoke.

"Chloe?" the Big E said in a voice softer than she'd ever heard. "Is that you?"

She felt a lump in her throat and swallowed hard.

"Yes," she said, "it's me."

She held her breath until she heard the words that she knew were coming even before he said them.

"You'd better come," the Big E said. "You'd better come home."

Darlene and Josh Mulholland: A Family of Freaks?

(Excerpted from *Time* magazine)

Friends of Josh Mulholland remember a curious boy fixated on the idea of human oddities, an obsession he cultivated by buying rare books and videos detailing human anomalies.

According to some, it was a terrible day in Darlene's life the day she discovered his collection.

"When she saw all the freaks," said one friend, "she freaked."

Others maintain that Josh's obsession was well-known in the family, and that he'd been known to draw comic strips of a family of deformed people modeled on the Mulhollands.

"He drew his mother with one eye, his father with a foot-long toe, and Darlene with a giant head," said one source. "He said they were all aliens. They all found it kind of funny."

The same friend recalls a time when Josh slapped Darlene for snooping in his collection.

"He whacked her a good one, like brothers do with little sisters," said the friend, "and told her never to go through his personal things again."

A childhood friend of Darlene's might be called to testify, as she apparently was the only other person to speculate about the pregnancy. According to the friend, Darlene confessed to imagining that the fetus growing inside her was some unknown part of her that had dislodged itself in her womb and taken refuge there, like a woman she'd seen in one of her brother's books who had teeth and bits of skull bones in her ovaries, as well as the leftover eye of a misbegotten twin floating along her lower intestine.

The house was dark when Chloe arrived. Even the night light had been switched off, the one her mother always kept burning in the hallway to keep Aunt Chickie from stumbling as she made her way to the medicine cabinet for Desitin to soothe her chafed legs during the night. Chloe remembered how she'd once thought that having a night light in her room might have saved her, that the slightest possibility of Irv's shadow being seen on the wall would have kept him away.

She left the Bubba doll in the trunk and lit a cigarette, the flame illuminating the lines of her thumb. If the party was under way, she couldn't understand why the house was so dark. She'd expected to find it blazing with lights, all of them milling about the living room while Irv shook off the last bits of his infancy, Ruth finally giving into her hunger by wolfing down bowls of Spider-Man Jell-O decorated with sugary webs. Even the Big E would participate, gulping whiskey and flexing his muscles while their mother snapped photographs, the flash lighting up the room.

With the cigarette poised between her fingers, she walked across the street and fumbled with her keys at the front door. If anyone were within earshot they'd have heard the jingling at the door, the impatient curses under her breath. Finally she turned the key in the lock and flung open the door.

Nathan pulled her close and switched on the kitchen light, his breath moist against her scalp.

"I knew you'd come," he said. "I knew you couldn't miss a performance like this."

They were running behind schedule, Nathan explained, taking her by the hand and leading her into the living room. He snapped on a tape recorder which played a recording of Aunt Chickie singing "Happy Birthday" over and over again in a voice painfully off-key. The kitchen was in disarray, the table covered in opened Jell-O boxes with powder spilling out the sides, a half-frosted cake with red smears sitting in the middle of the table. Beside the cake sat a bag of streamers, a roll of Scotch tape balanced precariously on the edge. Five plastic Spider-Man masks stared up at her.

Her mother bustled around the living room with packages of party favors emblazoned with Spider-Man's face, setting them on end tables and on top of the television. She nodded when she saw Chloe and handed her several of the packets, candy Spider-Man heads spilling all over the floor.

"Did you get the Spidey whistles?" her mother asked as they leaned down to pick up the candy. "Nathan said you drove all the way home to find them."

Chloe looked up at Nathan who gave her a conspiratory wink.

"No," she said. "I mean, I tried everywhere, but I just couldn't find them."

Flo smiled, her eyes crinkling at the corners.

"That's okay," her mother said. "The important thing is that you tried for our boy."

Chloe shoved the candy back into the bags and tossed several onto the sofa. Whenever Nathan threw parties, he always created the illusion of having more guests than were actually present. He instructed Chloe and her mother to leave the bags of party favors everywhere, even in the bathroom.

"Let him find Spidey wherever he turns," he said. "We'll hit him right where he lives."

Aunt Chickie huffed through the living room with a tray of red and white cupcakes. Even the Big E was in party mode, standing on a chair and securing streamers to the corners of the living room ceiling with multicolored Scotch tape. Nathan stood feeding the streamers to the Big E in loops as he twisted them in curls with both hands.

"Well," Chloe asked Nathan as she left the last of the packages of favors near the basement door, "is he back?"

He lowered the streamers and called to the Big E in an encouraging voice.

"You're doing a fine job, E," Nathan said, "some of the best damn streamer work I've ever seen."

The Big E gave Nathan a thumbs-up and continued to paw at the streamers with his taped fingers.

"We don't know," Nathan whispered. "No one's been down to check on him. I think even your mother is afraid to look."

Chloe stood in the living room watching as her mother brought out trays of red M & M's and sprinkled red confetti over the carpet.

"Chloe," Ruth said, stumbling toward her, "I knew you'd come back."

Ruth embraced her, her heavy belly against Chloe's middle. They stood that way for a long time as Chloe closed her eyes, pressing herself harder against Ruth's belly to try to feel the life inside her.

When Ruth finally released her, the flash of a camera sent orange spots shooting through Chloe's eyes.

"Say 'Happy Birthday,'" her mother said, snapping another photo, and as Ruth reached for a cupcake on a nearby tray, Chloe found herself saying it through gritted teeth.

When the last of the streamers had been hung and the Green Goblin Jell-O mold had hardened and cooled enough to eat, they took their places in the living room to wait for Irv's reappearance. At first Aunt Chickie fretted over leaving Irv unattended for such a long period of time, but Nathan insisted that, like the party, his reentry should be a surprise.

Flo sat on the arm of the recliner next to the Big E, who had changed into his green tank top in honor of this special occasion. Her brow sweated and she winced from time to time, twitching in her seat.

"He'll be all right soon enough," her mother said, clasping the Big E's taped hand and grimacing. She took several deep breaths and blew out her rounded mouth. "The boy will be all right," she added, brightening. "A mother knows these things."

Nathan switched on the tape recorder and helped Ruth to a sitting position next to Chloe where Ruth ate cupcakes and held her belly with her free hand. He brought a tray around to the others, though they all refused the cupcakes, all except for Aunt Chickie, who ate one slowly, her lips smacking.

"It's not the best version I've ever done," Aunt Chickie said, wiping crumbs away with a tissue from her bra strap, "but Ralph always did like my singing. I was glad to do it in a pinch."

Nathan smiled over at Chloe, but she didn't smile back. She knew this was how Nathan behaved during parties, ever the host, with his ingratiating smile and willingness to please. It was one of the things she loved most about him, his ability to slip so easily into this role, to find something to celebrate in everything, yet she found she couldn't watch him behave this way in front of her family without feeling a knot in her stomach.

After nearly an hour of sitting and staring at each other, the silence punctuated only by the sounds of her mother's strained breathing and the periodic replaying of Aunt Chickie's voice, everyone seemed on edge. No sounds came from the basement, and the Green Goblin Jell-O mold began to dissolve in the heat. The Big E grunted and rubbed at his biceps. His patience was wearing thin, Chloe could see by the look on his face. Ruth patted absently at Chloe's arm and wiped at the sweat that was now pouring down her face. Chloe thought someone should offer to get her a glass of water, but she made no move to get it herself.

"Okay, everyone," Nathan said, getting to his feet and clapping his hands. "It's time for a change of plan."

Before Chloe could ask him what he was thinking, he ran to the kitchen and came back carrying the Spider-Man masks in one hand and a crepe paper web in the other. One by one he handed out the masks, then dangled the web from the knot of streamers in the middle of the room.

"It would really be something," Aunt Chickie whispered to Chloe, "if he came back as Peter Parker after all this."

Chloe smiled but said nothing, forcing herself to bite into one of the chocolate Spider-Men. She nipped at its neck and then spit a wad of chocolate into a napkin.

"Don't put too much weight on those streamers," the Big E said. "I'm not putting those goddamned things up again, even if somebody rises from the dead."

Nathan persuaded them all to put their masks on in unison. Ruth slid hers over her face immediately then turned to look at Chloe, her eyes shining through the white plastic sockets of the mask.

"Ralph used to make me wear this," she whispered through her mask, "when we first got married."

Chloe turned away and pulled the mask over her own face.

"Okay, now we need it to be darker in here," Nathan said, reaching up to close the heavy drapes on the backyard window. "Spidey likes the dark."

The room grew suddenly quiet. The tape recorder snapped itself off, Aunt Chickie's voice ending on a particularly painful suspended "you" in the "happy birthday" refrain. Chloe's breath whistled inside the plastic mask. The room was so dark it was difficult to tell who was who.

"What should we do?" someone whispered, and then Ruth began to heave in her seat, her whole body lurching forward as she struggled to hold on to Chloe's arm.

She tumbled to the floor, one of the dessert trays crashing as she fell. Chloe tried to lift her mask to see what was happening, but the elastic seemed suddenly tighter, as if her head had swelled. She felt Aunt Chickie grabbing her by the arms, a tangle of bodies and Spider-Man masks struggling on the floor.

"Get the lights! Get the lights!" someone shrieked, but no one seemed able to find the switch, the sound of party bags being torn apart rising in the room.

"For Christ's sake, Ruth, get hold of yourself!" Chloe heard the Big E shout, and then the web fell from the ceiling, all of the streamers floating down over his head. She heard them shredding, the Big E cursing in a loud voice as Ruth's cries grew louder.

"Oh, God, he's coming!" she moaned. "My baby's coming!"

Aunt Chickie grabbed hold of Chloe's arm and squeezed it, her fingernails digging into Chloe's flesh. Chloe wanted to tell her to let go, but before she could say anything, Aunt Chickie fell against her in her effort to get up from the couch. Chloe felt the wind knocked out of her and pushed at Aunt Chickie with all of her might, her hands sinking into the doughy flesh of Chickie's back. Ruth's moans reached a fierce crescendo. Aunt Chickie rocked back and forth as she tried to force herself up, but she wouldn't budge, no matter how hard Chloe struggled.

Chloe closed her eyes and pressed herself against the back of the couch. The mask cut into her face, elastic stabbing above her ears and in the back of her head. She wriggled her body and managed to free one leg. She lifted her foot and pressed it into Aunt Chickie's back as hard as she could.

"Please," Chloe said in a strangled voice, "get off me."

Suddenly the weight lifted, the air surging in Chloe's lungs. When she opened her eyes, Aunt Chickie lay sprawled on the floor, her chafed legs in the air. The Big E held his fists up as if ready to ward off an attack, the mask torn from his face and crumpled at his feet.

Nathan switched on the lights and ran for his index cards and Cross pen.

"He's coming," Ruth wheezed, "I feel him coming."

The Big E began shouting commands for hot water and towels, a pillow for Ruth's head. Chloe bent between Ruth's legs and draped a blanket over her knees. Carefully she eased Ruth's underpants and leggings down, cushioning her bottom in a layer of white bath towels Aunt Chickie had brought her. Just as she slid them off, Ruth's water broke, soaking Chloe in a whoosh of thick brown water.

"Someone call an ambulance!" Aunt Chickie yelled, but before she waited for anyone to respond, she hurried into the kitchen to make the call herself.

Chloe crouched down with her head under the blanket. Fluid swirled into the towels beneath Ruth's buttocks, knots of blood and pain, the opening a deep red wound. She thought she saw the head but couldn't be sure.

"He's coming!" Ruth moaned again. "My boy is coming!"

Chloe pulled her head out from under the blanket and looked at her father standing there, the tape hanging helplessly from his fingers.

"Where's Mom?" she asked. "Mom's the only one who's had a baby."

As Chloe crouched between Ruth's legs, she felt the familiar grip of fear in her chest that her mother had vanished. She'd always known that if she turned her back one too many times, her mother would creep away silently, leaving Chloe behind.

"Good Christ," the Big E shouted, backing away in his squeamishness, "where the hell is Flo?"

She looked up at Aunt Chickie, who was holding the portable phone out to her like an offering.

"The ambulance is on its way," Aunt Chickie said, puffing. "Here, hon, take the phone and help that poor girl."

Chloe said nothing as Ruth began to cry, soft whimpers at first, but then growing louder and louder, the screams filling the room. Nathan thrust an index card in her face.

"Not now," Chloe told him. "Now is not the time."

Ruth writhed in pain on the floor, her hands moving between her legs as she rocked back and forth. Chloe heard the operator talking to her as if through a tunnel of water. Yes, she thought she could see the head, and yes, there seemed to be time, though how she knew this she wasn't sure. Screams reverberated through the room until Chloe was sure they were coming from inside her own head.

Suddenly she realized that the screams were sirens, that the ambulance had arrived. Men ran frantically toward them, scooping up the towels and moving Ruth onto the stretcher. As they hurried through the living room, a webbed band of streamers caught on Chloe's feet. She kicked them away, tearing the streamers into bits.

"It's all right now, Ruth, they're going to take care of you," Nathan said, his hand on the side of the stretcher. "They'll know just what to say."

He handed her a packet of index cards as the Big E grabbed one side of the stretcher and hoisted Ruth into the ambulance.

"You take these if you need them," he said. "Don't be afraid to say any of it."

Ruth nodded and closed her eyes against the pain. The Big E got in beside her, crouching down on one of the seats as if ready for a lift.

"Go find your mother!" he shouted above the sirens, but before Chloe could answer, the doors of the ambulance slammed shut, and she was left there with a cloud of exhaust rushing over her, the lights leaving bright yellow spots when she closed her eyes. When she opened them again, she found Nathan standing beside her with an index card in his hand. Without a word, he slipped the card to her and traced his finger over the block lettering.

IRV'S GONE, the index card read. IRV'S GONE.

Homecoming Queen's Day of Reckoning

Associated Press

Long Island, NY

A grand jury indicted former homecoming queen Darlene Mulholland yesterday on two counts of reckless endangerment of a minor and one count of abandonment. District Attorney Madreski said that the state will file charges of either first or second degree murder if the body of infant "Bubba" is recovered in the next few days.

"We want to send a message to all teenagers," said Madreski, "that a locker room is no place to leave a baby."

After instituting an Island-wide search, Greenleaf Point police chief Carl Robinson said that there were no new leads as to Bubba's whereabouts.

"We have some bloody towels and an umbilical cord," Robinson said in a terse statement to the press, "but, as we all know, that could mean anything."

Mulholland defense counsel Lawrence Englebaum refused to answer questions regarding Darlene Mulholland's state of mind, though he reiterated claims of his client's innocence and said there would be no murder charges filed without a corpus delicti.

"They have no body," Englebaum said, "because there is no body to be found. Bubba is alive. He was stolen, just as my client has always maintained. The courts will vindicate her. We are confident of that."

Surrounding communities have organized search parties to aid in the desperate attempt to find Bubba. Sagamore High School students combed the area surrounding the school grounds until dawn.

When asked why groups of students have organized rallies to raise money for Mulholland's defense, one student said, "She's our queen. Nothing can change that."

Mulholland was stripped of her crown a short time after it was discovered that she had abandoned the infant Bubba in the girls' locker room at Sagamore High. No new queen has been named.

Chloe's first thought was that her mother had taken him. She imagined her mother with the blanketed Irv strapped in the passenger seat, his giant head bouncing against the leather seats whenever she accidentally ran over curbs in her hurry to keep Irv from being found. As she sat smoking on the backyard bench, Chloe wondered if her mother had known the same kind of desperation the homecoming queen had felt, if she'd taken Irv and left him somewhere because no one would ever understand him. She wondered if her mother had left him in a pile of blankets and booties, if all of her misguided mother love had forced her to make the ultimate sacrifice by hiding him away. No one would have blamed her, Chloe thought, not if they had seen Irv with his bulbous head and shrinking bluish lips.

Chloe took a deep breath and tossed her cigarette into the tomato garden. Maybe the embers wouldn't die, she thought. Maybe it would all burn. Sometimes she had nightmares about flames licking the windows, her mother's face turned to ash. Afterward, she'd sit with her charcoal pencil and try to reconstruct her mother's face on paper, but inevitably she made the nose too broad, the chin too pointed, the brow line too thick. Even in the pieces of leftover dreams, her mother's face eluded her.

As soon as she heard Aunt Chickie calling her name, she knew her mother had been found. In fact, as she dragged herself into the house and down the basement steps, Aunt Chickie's voice ringing in her ears, she realized that her mother's escape would be impossible. No matter what happened, no matter what Irv had done, she knew that her mother would remain steadfast, laughing at his trips to the bathroom, standing guard at his bassinet.

"Mom," she said, when she found her mother huddled in a rocking chair next to the empty bassinet.

It was a statement, not a question. *Mother, father, brother, sister,* Chloe thought, standing there in the basement while her mother rocked. This was who they were.

Her mother looked up from the rocking chair and stared at Chloe. All at once her features seemed to crumple in on themselves, her nose and mouth seeming to fuse, the lines under her eyes and down her neck twisting in on themselves. Chloe moved her eyes across the contours of her mother's face. She'd always had a thick and knotted look about her. The curve of her mother's mouth pursed and bent.

No wonder she'd never been able to draw her mother. She did not know who she was.

"They'll think I did this," Flo said suddenly, standing up and sending the rocking chair backward with a loud scrape. "They'll think I took him."

Perhaps this once, Chloe thought, her mother would speak directly.

"Who will think that?" she asked, moving closer to her mother. "Why would anyone think that?"

Before Chloe could reach out to touch her mother's arm, her mother swung forward and out of reach.

"They always blame the mother," she said. "Look at that homecoming queen. That girl is in jail, even though that's just where she belongs, and everyone wants to know where her mother was when this happened. No one even mentions the father."

Her mother bent over the bassinet and fussed with the blankets now tangled in knots. The white sheet was frayed at the ends, the plastic crucifix dangling from the nail on the wall. The impression of Irv's head remained curved into the pillow.

"Mom," Chloe said softly, "what are you talking about?"

Her mother fingered the pillow and sighed.

"He's my boy," she said. "He's still my boy."

She fluffed the pillow with both hands, the bassinet creaking with the weight of her movements.

"What else would you have me do?" she asked, and before Chloe could answer, Aunt Chickie called to them from the top of the stairs.

"They've got him!" she yelled. "They've found Ralph!"

Flo dropped the pillow and hurried past Chloe, not looking back once as she climbed the stairs as quickly as she could. Chloe watched her shadow move along the wall and up the stairs until the door opened, and her mother was gone again.

No one dared complain about Nathan's crazed driving on the way to the hospital, least of all Chloe. She simply wrapped her right hand around the strap hanging by the window and smoked with her left hand. Horns blared, drivers swore, but Nathan refused to slow down.

When they pulled up in front of the hospital, Aunt Chickie's head banged the front seat and then snapped back again.

"She's all right," Flo said, even though no one had made any comment. She swung the car door open and hurried ahead. "We've got to get my boy."

Chloe stepped out of the car and saw the crowd of people gathered. Her mother was already gone, swallowed up by the throngs of people, but she did not call her mother's name or even try to find her. Nathan took Aunt Chickie by one arm and waved Chloe ahead.

"Look!" he called, as she moved closer to the crowd of people looking up at one of the buildings. "He's up on the wall."

Craning her neck, Chloe caught sight of the sheets tied in knots hanging from a window frame, a body suspended with its feet pressed against the bricks, hands wrapped tightly around the tangled sheet. She was about to duck behind a security guard when Irv turned toward her. His eyes were painted black around the edges, the rest of his face colored a dark red.

"It's Irv," she said aloud. "Irv's hanging out the window."

"Irv?" the guard asked. "I thought his name was Ralph."

Nathan pushed his way beside Chloe and began scribbling on his index cards.

"Don't ask," he said to the guard. He passed him an index card and patted him on the back. "Here, try this line."

The guard squinted at the index card and then looked up at Nathan.

"Who's Chloe?" he asked, shoving the card back at Nathan. "And why would this guy want to play bingo when he's trying to kill himself, for crying out loud?"

Chloe let go of Nathan and leaned her head back to look up at Irv again. Even from a height of roughly eighty feet, she could see the fear in his eyes even beneath the black circles and dark red paint masking his face.

She stood there listening to the sirens as a crush of faces began to press themselves against her. She wondered where her mother was, why she wasn't screaming his name above the crowd. She watched him swinging in the air from the bedsheets, his mouth open, head thrown back.

"He's not trying to kill himself," Chloe said sadly. "He wants to be Spidey."

"I thought that's what he was trying to do," one of the guards said. "Check it out. He's trying to scale the wall."

With the megaphone in hand, the guard barked orders for the crowd to move back, to give them room.

"Are you Chloe?" a man asked. "Are you his sister?"

She felt the weight of Nathan's hand on her back as he slipped an index card to her.

"Yes," she said. "I am."

A psychiatrist shouted questions at her, but Chloe heard them only as background noise, like static between radio stations. If they would all just be quiet, she thought, she might be able to think of what to do.

"Okay, Chloe," the guard said, showing her how to operate the megaphone, "try not to upset him if you can help it. Just speak calmly and hold this button when you want to talk."

She nodded and looked back at Nathan, who shuffled nervously through his cards.

"This one maybe," he muttered, "no, no, maybe this one."

He shrugged his shoulders helplessly and dropped his hands to his sides.

"You can do it," he said. "He'll listen to you."

He leaned forward and squeezed her hand. She nodded and stepped out in front of the crowd. If she could only light a cigarette, she thought frantically, she could become Esther Bing. Esther Bing was the kind of woman who would help him. Esther Bing would know what to say. But she could not be Esther Bing now, not with so many people watching. She could only be Chloe and pray that Chloe would think of something to say. She closed her eyes and thought of Ruth's baby sliding into the world, safe in his incubator.

"Irv," she said, her voice echoing out across the courtyard, "it's me. It's Chloe."

The crowd quieted as she moved closer to the window where Irv dangled. Her lips felt sewn together like one of her dolls, and she thought how cruel bingo had been to so many of them.

"Irv," she said again, and then in a louder voice, "Ralph."

He turned to look at her then and smiled, the red makeup crinkling on his face. His knees were bent as his sneakers pressed against the wall of the hospital. A group of policemen leaned over the side of a fire escape, reaching to try to grab his torso as he swung toward them.

"Chloe," he called out, "is that you?"

He pushed off the building with both feet. The sheet twirled over his head, his body spinning in midair before sliding down and then landing against the building again. The crowd gasped as he hung in the balance then sighed as his feet touched the bricks.

"Hey," he shouted, turning, "look at me, Chloe! I'm Spidey!"

She clicked the megaphone button to speak but no words would come. What if she said the wrong thing? What if he let go? She jumped up on her tiptoes to see past the growing crowd, but she couldn't find any of them, not Nathan, not Aunt Chickie, and least of all, her mother.

"Chloe!" he yelled, pushing off the building, "I'm Spidey! I know all about Spidey, don't you see?"

She wiped her nose with the back of her hand.

"Yes, Ralph," she said. "I see."

The policemen from the floor below leaned out the window in their attempt to grab his legs. *Don't move too fast,* she wanted to say. *Don't scare him.* A rescue team scrambled across the courtyard as he swung back and forth, the sheet bucking with his weight.

"Remember how we used to sing?" Irv screamed, throwing his head back. "Do you remember, Chloe?"

He swung out from the building again, eyes closed, knees bending with the force of his body crashing into the building.

"Let's sing it, okay?" she heard Irv say in a voice that had long ago disappeared into the depths of their childhood, a voice of lazy Saturday mornings watching television with their dog Gretchen between them, a voice that had belonged to a boy who loved Spider-Man, a boy who watched cartoons and who had a little sister. She could see them there, sitting on the living room floor in their pajamas as they waited for their favorite superhero to come on. She'd once loved Spidey, too. How had she forgotten?

"Sing, Chloe, sing!" Irv called, and she clicked the megaphone on, letting her voice ring over the crowd, as loud and off-key as Aunt Chickie's rendition of "Happy Birthday."

She saw them there on the carpet as they sang, over and over again until Chloe's voice was hoarse, her throat burning with the effort to keep singing. Irv belted the chorus one last time, and then his whole body shook as the policemen caught hold of his feet. He was too quick for them, though, arching his back to swing away. His shoe dropped with a loud crack to the concrete. The policemen lunged forward to reach him, but he was hanging too far away from the building.

"Chloe! Chloe!" he shrieked. "Help me!"

She heard the sound of the sheet tearing as he spun in the air, the screams of the crowd all around her. She clicked the megaphone button and said the first thing that came to mind.

"Irv," she said with as much force as she could muster, "it's time for you to stop this. Go on in now. You've got to stop this."

He looked down at her, and for one brief moment, she saw him again as a little boy, but different this time, not as a lonely boy with only a superhero for a friend, but as the little boy who had been her brother years ago and then had become a stranger. The brother she'd come to know as "Irv the Perv." She didn't know who this Irv was, this Irv hanging in the balance, and she didn't want to know him. She only wanted him to get inside.

Policemen on both sides reached for his arms at once and held him, his arms outstretched as they held him up there, his body dangling, head hanging down. The crowd let out a long gasp as Chloe looked up at Irv hanging there, suspended, the policeman's hands curved under his armpits, his head jerking as they tried to pull him in the window.

"Okay," she heard a faint voice say, and then he disappeared inside the window, the policemen's hands cradling his back and neck. The torn sheet floated down over the crowd, and she moved away and lowered the megaphone before letting go. It flipped over on itself and then fell to the ground.

Chloe and Nathan were ushered into a small security office at the opposite end of the hospital for word on Irv's condition. Despite the no smoking policy, a security guard named Holter lit Chloe's cigarettes for her and sprayed the air with Lysol to mask the smell. He was a reformed smoker himself, he said, though stunts such as these always brought the urge for nicotine back to him full force.

"Like I'd never quit," he said, fingering another cigarette before handing it to Chloe. She shakily placed it between her lips as he leaned over to light it. "Nothing like watching a grown man dying to be Spider-Man to make you want a Marlboro more than anything."

The psychiatrist handed her several forms to sign in order for Irv to be examined by the doctors. Since Ruth was still groggy from giving birth and her mother would not leave Irv's side in the emergency room, Chloe was asked to offer her signature. How odd it was to see those words printed so boldly—next of kin. She placed her cigarette in the ashtray and skimmed over the papers, the words swirling together.

"Chloe," the psychiatrist asked as she gripped the pen, "can you tell me anything more about your brother that might be relevant to what's happened? Do you have any idea why he'd want to become Spider-Man?"

She stubbed out the cigarette and leaned her head back against the seat. She thought about the times they'd sat in front of the television as kids, the glow in Irv's eyes whenever Spidey appeared, whenever poor, retiring Peter Parker gave way to the stealthy superhero. Of course she might have said any number of things: that somehow watching Spidey scale walls gave Irv a feeling of power he'd never been able to achieve in his ordinary life, that he'd locked himself in a bathroom and stolen their father's girlie magazines only to be talked out by a priest. She might have told the psychiatrist about his visits to her bedroom, about his attempts to become an infant again, their mother's constant coddling.

"I really couldn't tell you," she said finally, which seemed to her the truest thing she could offer.

The psychiatrist nodded and exchanged a knowing look with Nathan. He seemed satisfied by this answer and said that new fathers often behaved oddly after the birth of sons. It was a kind of displacement anxiety, he said, an unseating of the throne. Some men handled it better than others. With careful attention and nurturing, the psychiatrist said, Irv would be back to normal in no time at all.

She felt Nathan's hand on her shoulder, pressing down gently as she signed her name in a loopy script next to the X. Esther Bing, she began to write, then crossed it out violently with the black fountain pen before signing Chloe Taft. In smaller, careful letters under the word "relationship" she wrote: sister.

Mulholland Brother Seen With Strange Woman; League for Disabilities Stages Protest

Associated Press

Long Island, NY

A neighbor claims to have seen Josh Mulholland, brother of Darlene, the homecoming queen who abandoned her infant at Sagamore High School, leaving the Mulholland family home with an unidentified woman some time after midnight.

The woman arrived carrying a bundle of white towels under one arm. She stayed only minutes at the Mulholland home before leaving with Josh in a black Mustang. Onlookers say the woman wore a long black skirt that seemed to protrude from her waist.

"Like she was hiding something," one neighbor said, "but what, I have no idea."

The League for People with Disabilities staged a protest in front of the courthouse yesterday because of what they believe is an unfair depiction of the disabled.

"If [Bubba] was born with anomalies," said one spokesperson, "then the media and Darlene Mulholland have sent a message that being different is something to run away from."

Attorneys speculate that what has now been dubbed the "freak defense" will be held inadmissible by the court.

Her mother had suffered a mild case of shock after witnessing Irv hanging from the window. Chloe hadn't known what had happened to her mother and was relieved to hear that she would fully recover, though the doctor refused to be more specific.

"Does she still speak in non sequiturs?" Nathan asked.

Chloe glared at him and thanked the doctor for his time.

"Feel free to go in and see the baby while you wait," the doctor said. "Ruth has been advised against the baby's rooming in with her because she needs her rest right now. He'll be in the nursery in Labor & Delivery, just down the hall. It may be a while until you can see your mother, and babies can be just the right thing in stressful times like these."

Of course, Chloe thought. The baby. With all Irv had put them through that day, she'd forgotten all about him.

Although she didn't want to see Irv or even Ruth, Chloe was surprised at how anxious she was to see the baby. Seeing Ruth so soon after giving birth would have unnerved her. In the past few weeks she'd gotten used to the sight of Ruth hugely pregnant, her belly swelling down over her pelvis and up to her breasts. Now that she'd given birth she would seem oddly deflated, Chloe thought, the life inside her having spilled itself out.

She went in with Nathan when it was their turn, the two of them walking briskly down the corridor to the nursery. They were both breathing heavily. At the large glass window they stooped in synch and leaned in closer, Nathan's face so close to the window that a small fogged cloud appeared in the glass before him.

"Which one is he?" Nathan asked, as Chloe searched the cards pasted to the incubators to find him. A sea of babies in white blankets trimmed in blue and pink stripes swam before her eyes before she spotted their name in the corner.

"There," she said, pointing. "There he is."

He had a full head of black hair that stuck upward from the top of his head. She felt an immense relief that the hair was straight, no curls on the top or hanging down over the brow. His nose crinkled as he moved his head from side to side as if feeling his way for his thumb tucked inside the jumper or for the breast he'd been denied by being taken away from his mother.

Irving Ralph Taft, the tag said in black printed letters. Six pounds, three ounces, 19.2" long.

"Holy Christ," Nathan said. "She named him Irv."

Chloe couldn't believe it herself. She leaned forward and squinted to make sure the name was right. Perhaps they'd inverted the two names by mistake, she thought, moving the name Ralph to the middle. Hospitals made mistakes all the time.

When a nurse passed by, Chloe stopped her at the window and gestured toward the infant.

"Excuse me," she said, smiling at the nurse to hide the shock she was feeling, "but I think they got my nephew's name wrong. I think they changed the order of his name."

The nurse shook her head at Chloe but said she would check her records to make sure.

"Which one's your nephew?" the nurse asked.

"Taft," Chloe said, grabbing hold of Nathan's hand. "The one in the corner."

The nurse peered in at the babies and raised her eyebrows.

"Oh, of course," she said. "He's the smallest one here." She laughed. "I don't know what they're feeding these women, but lately all we seem to get are ten-pounders."

While they waited for the nurse to return, Nathan kept staring in at the baby with his forehead pressed to the glass. He couldn't imagine what Ruth had been thinking, he said, to give the baby a name that Flo had always hated.

The nurse tapped Chloe on the shoulder with a copy of the birth certificate.

"See, there's been no mistake," she said. "Irving Ralph, just like it says. See here, it has the raised seal? That makes it official."

Chloe thanked her and muttered under her breath that she still believed something had gone wrong in the naming.

"I don't blame you," the nurse said before turning to walk away. "They'll call him Irv for sure."

Though no one would confirm her suspicions, Chloe believed that Ruth had named the baby "Irv" as an act of revenge, or at least as a comeuppance for what Irv had put her through. When she'd first met the family, she'd asked Chloe why she called her brother "Irv" when his real name was Ralph, and out of respect, Chloe had tried to stop doing so for a time, at least in front of Ruth.

"Irv," Ruth would say, her face turning pink with laughter. "It gets me every time."

As far as Chloe knew, Irv had never expressed any outward distaste for the nickname. He'd agreed to give it to his son, though Chloe suspected that decision had more to do with guilt or compliance after his episode as an infant than with any real affection for a nickname that had been born of disdain. He must have known Chloe called him "Irv" as a mockery. Perhaps he thought he deserved it.

"They named him Irv," Nathan said again as they headed out toward the exit. "Imagining naming your kid Irv."

He shook his head and laughed. Chloe found herself laughing, too, short hiccuping snorts that started in her upper chest and made her lightheaded.

Later she and Nathan waited in the lobby for word on her mother's condition. Irv had been calm enough to be permitted to see his new son, the doctors had said, though he'd continued to mumble incoherently even after several injections of Valium.

"If I didn't know better I'd think he was reciting bingo numbers mixed together with the Hail Mary," she heard one of the doctors whisper, "though what that has to do with Spider-Man, I haven't the slightest notion."

Finally a doctor from the cardiac wing arrived to tell them that her mother was out of danger. She was sitting up in bed and seemed in good spirits, he said, though she had not stopped asking about Irv.

"More than anything else, she wants to see her son," the doctor said. "All she needs is to see her boy, she says, but of course that will have to wait until your brother is a bit more stable."

She and Nathan glanced at each other and laughed softly to themselves, the kind of nervous laughter that often arises in traumatic situations, the psychiatrist said.

There really was nothing funny about it, she thought, as the laughter bubbled up in her chest and burst forth from her mouth, an open-mouthed laughter that left her shaking. Their shoulder blades clanged together as they laughed without making a sound. Of course the doctors didn't share in the joke and smiled sadly down at them as if pitying their lack of feeling on Irv's behalf.

"Pinch my leg," Chloe choked, as the laughter racked their bodies, and he did, so hard that later a series of small purple bruises appeared on the back of her knee, just inside the crook. She knew that in the days to come she would have to stand naked in front of the mirror with her long calf sloping down to see the marks that had been left there, violet spirals of blood that swelled up under her skin.

In the midst of their laughter, the doctor told them that they could finally visit with her mother. They could only stay a few minutes, the doctor said apologetically, though Chloe assured him that would be more than enough time.

"All she needs is rest and some fluids," the doctor said as he led them to the hospital room. "That, of course, and to see her boy, as she calls him, though I wouldn't advise that at this time."

Chloe thanked the doctor, amazed that she was able to carry on pleasantries with people as if nothing had happened.

"Well, well, look who's here," Aunt Chickie said, struggling up from her chair to kiss first Nathan and then Chloe, leaving bright magenta lipstick prints on both of their faces. Chloe wiped Nathan's away with her thumb but stopped him from reciprocating. She rather liked the idea of carrying a mark, a kind of souvenir for the day. "I'll bet you two are just starved."

The Big E got up to greet them and patted them both on the shoulders. His red tank top was frayed at the neckline, the tape around his fingers hanging in crazy swirls. When Nathan asked him what Ruth had said during labor, the Big E tilted his head back and closed his eyes to think.

"She said it hurt like hell and that she was glad it was a boy," he said. "Other than that, mostly she just screamed."

Nathan nodded and wrote some notes on one of his index cards.

"How did you know she was glad it was a boy?" Aunt Chickie asked, her words slurred through the chicken in her mouth.

"Because that's what she said," the Big E responded. "She said, 'I'm so glad it's a boy.'"

He pulled up chairs for each of them and stuffed his mouth with a chicken leg from the bucket on her mother's bedside table.

"Not too original, I know," the Big E whispered to Nathan, "but I got the hell out of there long before the baby came. I wasn't about to give her any lines."

Nathan laughed and sat in one of the chairs, pulling another close for Chloe to sit beside him.

"We ordered Kentucky Fried Chicken, extra crispy and regular," Aunt Chickie said. "I had no idea they delivered."

Nathan chose a leg and handed Chloe a breast, though she left hers sitting on a napkin in her lap. Flo smiled at them and wiped grease from her parted lips. She'd heard that Irv was safe, Aunt Chickie whispered, and that was all they were to tell her at this point.

"You brought him in," her mother said, setting her chicken bone on the tray across her bed and fluffing her hair with her fingers. "I told them nothing was wrong with my boy, that he was just overwrought with the baby coming."

With her fingers, Chloe picked at the chicken breast and nodded, digging with her fingernail into the hard coating and piercing the white skin that lay beneath it. The atmosphere was festive, with balloons tied to her mother's bedpost and the red-and-white carton of chicken in the middle of the table.

"I guess it's party time again," Nathan said with a mouthful of chicken, though Flo merely glanced at him and kept talking.

Flo wiped her fingers with some tissues Aunt Chickie handed to her and motioned for Chloe to approach the bed. Laying the food aside, Chloe got up noisily from the chair to her mother's side, gently letting her hip rest against the edge of the bed. Her mother's eyes were bright despite the dark circles beneath them, her arm bruised where the intravenous needle had penetrated her skin.

"Tell me," her mother whispered, taking one of Chloe's hands in hers and pulling her closer, "what did you say to bring your brother in? I couldn't hear with all those people." She smacked her lips together as Chloe stared into the doughy face that had so often eluded her. If she would ever draw her mother, she thought, if she could ever make a doll in her likeness, this was how she would depict her, pale and starved for bits of information about her son.

Chloe looked at Nathan who was busily gnawing at a chicken leg and laughing at something the Big E had said. She cleared her throat to get his attention for him to give her some cue of how to respond, but Nathan seemed not to have heard.

"He came in on his own," Chloe lied, staring down at her mother's hands, the slopes of her knuckles and long slender fingers. Sometimes she modeled the doll's hands after her mother's since they were so fine-boned and lovely, with a delicate pattern of veins and soft tendons stretched over with warm skin. "I didn't do much at all."

Her mother pulled Chloe toward her, resting Chloe's head against her breast.

"But you were there for him, and that's what counts," her mother said, then bent to kiss the top of her head. "You were there just like a sister should be."

As she lay against her mother's breast, Chloe felt hot tears pricking the sides of her eyes. She imagined that she were thirteen again and that her mother were consoling her on the bed next to the white hot daisies that stared at her through the night. She allowed herself to be lost in that moment, in the illusion that she was not in a hospital bed surrounded by the smells of chicken, but back in that bedroom where she'd needed her mother most, when there had been no one but Gretchen and her name in lilac above the bed.

Priest Finds Baby at Bingo Hall: Could This Be Bubba?

Associated Press

Long Island, NY

A priest at Saint Luke the Evangelical Church in Fairmouth, Long Island, reported finding an infant in the church's bingo hall last night at approximately 11:30 p.m.

Father Thomas McInnis, a priest at the parish for nearly ten years, found the infant resting in a blue basket in the bingo hall after being awakened at the nearby rectory shortly after retiring for the evening.

"I thought at first it was a cat trapped in the hall when I heard what sounded like mewing," Father McInnis said. "Instead it was a baby with a rather large head."

Father McInnis immediately aroused Monsignor Michaels and called the Department of Child Services some time after midnight.

The baby boy is said to weigh between fourteen and fifteen pounds and seemed well cared for, despite the largeness of the infant's skull.

"We'd all been praying for the lost infant for weeks," McInnis said, "and suddenly there he was, crying at the feet of Our Lord and Savior."

People who attended last night's bingo game say the evening was routine, with no evidence of an infant having been on the premises or remote traces of foul play.

"It took a long time for people to win the last couple of jackpots," said longtime bingo caller Henry Douglas. "We seemed to keep having the same numbers come up, and people were yelling that the fix was in, but what could I do? I only call them as I see them."

Mulholland family attorney Lawrence Englebaum refused to verify whether the woman seen late Thursday night leaving the Mulholland family home with Josh Mulholland had a third leg, as many neighbors have claimed.

There would be no good-byes. On the way out, Chloe stopped and hugged her father in the lobby. She smelled all the familiar smells she'd always loved about him—sweat, most of all, mixed with a rubbery smell that always reminded her of baseball mitts, though her father had never played the game. She would be in touch, she promised, and the Big E nodded and looked away.

"He's back now, and he's got a boy of his own," he said. "We'll see how long he cleaves."

He leaned over Nathan's shoulder to glance at the remaining index cards.

"You got any good ones in there for me?" the Big E asked. "I'm on my own now, for Christ's sake."

Nathan did an odd bow and presented him with some cards, then held out his hands, palms flat.

"That's the last of them, E," he said. "You just cleave, and you'll be all right."

The Big E nodded and stepped back toward the automatic doors. Chloe turned around to wave one last time, and as she did, the doors began opening and closing over and over again. People tried to move around him to get in or out of the hospital, but the Big E seemed not to notice, standing there in the doorway, waving to his daughter while the doors moved rhythmically behind him.

In the days that followed, Chloe and Nathan did little more than read newspapers and watch the news for updates on the results of Bubba's DNA testing. They kept the television on in their bedroom at night. Chloe hung articles on the clothesline in her work room and sat looking at them for a long time, swiveling on her stool. Nathan came in and found her among the snatches of batting she'd used for the Bubba doll. She smiled up at him, the flicker of the television screen throwing blue shadows across the room.

"It's Bubba," he said, touching her lightly on the shoulder. "They got the results."

He stroked her hair as she held the tufts of batting in her hands, the cotton fibers tickling her skin.

"I knew it," she said. "I just knew she wasn't lying. You don't lie about things like that."

They walked to their bedroom and sat together on the edge of the bed. A doctor in a white lab coat explained the process of matching Bubba's DNA to the frozen placenta that had been saved all these weeks.

"Although Darlene Mulholland has expressed her desire to have the baby returned to her," one reporter said, "the courts will decide what effects the abandonment of this infant will have in the long-term. Lawyers have speculated that the former homecoming queen will enter a guilty plea to avoid the stress of a lengthy trial."

When the camera panned to a picture of the infant Bubba being carried into the hospital followed by a pair of priests, Chloe stood up and shut the television off.

"Don't you want to see what happened?" Nathan asked, but she shook her head and lay down beside him on the bed. His knees curved against hers as they lay together like spoons. She brushed the remaining newspapers off the side of the bed and concentrated on the feel of his skin. Wiry hairs pricked the soft spot of her knee. She closed her eyes and mentally drew her name across the bed sheets: *Chloe, Chloe, Chloe.*

That night while Nathan lay sleeping beside her, Chloe slipped on her bathrobe and padded down the hall to her work room. Nathan had carried the box there for her when they'd unpacked, pausing only to shake the box before setting it down on her work table. Slowly she lifted the lid to inspect what she'd done. The work she'd done had been frantic, and part of her was frightened about what she might see when she looked at the doll again now that Irv was back and she no longer had to work in tiny snatches of time stolen from her parents' house. Normally she worked methodically with several dolls in different stages, reserving mornings for the details of a face and head, afternoons for the preliminary work necessary for shaping armatures or sketching new ideas. Often she couldn't get her ideas down quickly enough, and she was left to choose from the faces of the Bingo Ladies that stayed in her mind the longest.

She laid Bubba down on the table with his white towel stitched to his back, his eyes sewn closed against the brightness of the lamps that surrounded the room. The needlework was crude, she realized, as she inspected the tiny fingers and hands. She'd left out the nuance of skin tone just exposed to the air, the raw veins pulsating through the clenched hands. There was so much work to be done, she realized, as she began pulling stitches from his sides, tweaking out clumps of polyfill and scattering them over the table.

She worked almost constantly, pausing only to use the bathroom or to take naps on the cot she kept in a corner of the room. Nathan brought her cups of tea and packs of cigarettes every few hours, made her cheese sandwiches on whole wheat bread. Each time he came to her door, she covered the doll in a white sheet.

On the third day the phone began to ring. Her mother called several times, but Chloe let the machine answer it. Ruth's doctor had said the baby Irv was slightly jaundiced, though he was allowed to go home. He needed sunlight. The chafing between Aunt Chickie's legs had not stopped burning since the party, a fact her mother thought had been a sympathetic reaction to Ruth's giving birth. The Big E had bought her a tub of Desitin and had gone back to wearing his red tank top immediately after leaving the hospital. Irv, however, was still under observation.

"Your brother seems fine," her mother said into the answering machine. "He seems not to remember any of it, but these doctors just won't let him go."

Chloe lit a cigarette and blew smoke in the air over her mother's voice. For years she'd wondered whether Irv remembered coming into her room at night, how her eyes sprung open. She remembered. She remembered it all.

The last message on the machine came from Mrs. Mulholland. She spoke slowly and carefully, her voice trembling.

"I expect by now you know what's happened," she said, in a voice that smacked of bitterness. "I can't imagine wanting the doll at a time like this, not after what Darlene has done, not when they won't give him back to us."

Chloe rewound the message several times, listening to every word over and over again.

"I do thank you, Esther," Mrs. Mulholland said, "and I hope you'll be able to sell the doll after all. Someone's bound to want it."

When the tape ended Chloe hurried out to the front porch for the newspaper. It was just after dawn, and the light on the porch was still lit. She could hear Nathan snoring as she pulled the piles of newspapers that had collected there in the frenzied work of the past few days.

She took the newspapers to the kitchen and spread them across the table. Nathan shuffled groggily into the room, turned on the coffeemaker, and sat down beside her.

"There's news about Bubba," she said, and when he asked her how she knew, she opened the newspaper to the articles on the first three pages.

Together they leaned in to read them, their shoulders touching. The police had found several bloodstained terry cloth towels in a field several miles from Sagamore High School covered with dried bits of what might have been the remains of an umbilical cord. Bubba's DNA had matched both the shards of the umbilical cord and the frozen placenta. Still, the courts ruled, custody of Bubba would not be returned to the family until all charges against Darlene had been filed. Even though Bubba was alive, the family was said to have been in mourning since hearing the news. The front page showed a wide-eyed Darlene looking off into the distance as if not sure where she was.

Chloe pushed open the door to the work room and stood in the darkness for several minutes, Nathan's body in silhouette, his face framed by the light coming from the hallway. The corners of his mouth were turned down, his shoulders hunched. Without another word she switched on the overhead light and searched his face as he moved toward the table and stood over the Bubba doll.

"Oh, Chloe," he said, reaching down to finger the hands with tiny fingernails glued to the ends, the curved edges of the oversize head, the knot of black yarn for the umbilical cord. "I had no idea."

She wondered what he thought she'd been working on. Yet another Bingo Lady from her past with a stack of cards covered in blotted ink, a face tight with anticipation of a lucky number falling into the slot?

"You don't understand," she said. "I'd never have made it if I thought they wouldn't give him back to her."

She held the doll tightly to her chest and breathed in the linty smell of his head. Didn't anyone see? she wanted to ask. No matter what Darlene had done, no matter what mistakes she'd made, nothing ever stopped a child from wanting its mother.

Later that night she went into the work room to search for the Mulhollands' number. She at least wanted to express her sympathy. She was planning what she would say when the sound of a male voice on the other end startled her.

"Hello?" the voice said. When she didn't answer, he continued. "Who is this?" he asked.

She took in her breath at the sharpness in his voice.

"This is Esther Bing," she said, then cleared her throat before saying his name. "Josh."

When he didn't answer, she spoke again.

"It's you, isn't it?" she asked.

There was a long pause before he spoke again.

"Yes," he said, "it's me."

What she said next came out in a wild blur: she had made a doll, she said, and his mother didn't want it. She didn't believe Bubba should be kept from his mother. Before she could tell him how sorry she was, he cut her off in mid-sentence.

"I want it," he said. "I want Bubba."

They made arrangements to meet later that day at a church several blocks from the Mulholland home. He gave her careful directions and told her to come alone.

"Nobody knows me," he said. "The whole world thinks I'm some kind of freak."

She hadn't been inside a church since Irv's wedding when she'd been forced to stand as bridesmaid in a peach chiffon dress that scratched at her breasts and kept slipping off one shoulder. Father Merritt had been unable to perform the ceremony because of the wedding of a tithing member of the church, much to the Big E's dismay, and had been replaced by a young priest with moussed hair and a large overbite who had lisped throughout the marriage vows.

"He didn't say one goddamned word about cleaving to your wife," the Big E had said on the receiving line at the back of the church, pulling on his bow tie as if it were strangling him. "That boy will never learn to cleave now, you mark my words."

While waiting for Josh to arrive, Chloe stood at the back of the church as she'd promised. Candles flickered in glass jars on both sides of the church, a large statue of the Virgin Mary holding an infant Jesus beside the altar. She looked up at Christ's sooty feet crossed at the ankles and back at the innocent baby in the Virgin's arms. Although she knew the crucifixion was an integral part of the church's teachings, Chloe had always wondered why Christ was so often depicted at the end of His life when it was so much more pleasing to look at the sleeping babe in Mary's arms. The sight of Christ with his crown of thorns elicited pangs of sympathy, she didn't deny that, but who didn't love the baby Jesus?

She was sitting in the last pew when he came in. He was more handsome than the magazine pictures she'd seen of him in the grainy shots in newspapers of him staring up at the sky outside the Mulholland home. She watched him slide off his faded denim jacket and dab his forehead with holy water. His white T-shirt had faded purple streaks on the sleeves and around the middle as if he were unpracticed in the art of laundry. This made her smile. He wiped his hands on his pants before sliding in beside her.

"Are you Esther?" he asked, laying his denim jacket beside him and eyeing the box.

She nodded and reached out to shake his hand.

"Yes," she said. "But you can call me Chloe."

He smiled and leaned back against the pew, his arm stretched out to rest behind her.

"Chloe," he said softly. "That's a cool name."

When she didn't answer, he looked up at the stained glass ceiling and let out a long sigh.

"There was this three-legged woman named Chloe," he said. "She had this third leg that hung out of her stomach, and she would let it fall down over her skirt or leave buttons open so it could come out through her blouse," he said, smiling to himself. "Chloe was her real name. Somebody told her she should call herself Tina, but she never liked it. She even had the name Chloe tattooed on her third leg in the back of her knee so people couldn't see it, you know?"

His eyes closed briefly as if imagining the leg at that very moment, the curve of the knee and long sloping calf.

"Chloe was a much cooler name, much cooler than Tina," he said, "and she knew it."

He wet his lips and rubbed his hands together.

"Darlene wasn't afraid of Bubba," he said, turning to look at Chloe directly for the first time. She noticed flecks of gray in his blue eyes, the hint of a scar above his eyebrow. "That's not why she ran. She's seen people who look a lot stranger than Bubba. I oughta know."

Chloe reached for the box and handed it to Josh, who set it on his lap and stared down at it before running his hands over the sides.

"How much is it?" he asked after a long silence. "I brought some cash with me, you know, about five hundred."

For a minute Chloe said nothing, just sat looking at the baby Jesus on the altar, the look of peace on the Virgin's face.

"No charge," she said, waving the money away. "No charge for this doll."

He started to open the box, his thumbs tucked under the flaps, but Chloe lay a hand over his to stop him. She didn't want to see his reaction when he looked at the doll for the first time. Normally that was one of the great pleasures of selling a doll, that combination of surprise and wonder that came over people's faces when they first looked at something she had made.

"Show it to your sister," Chloe said, standing up to adjust her jacket. "Let her see it first."

They said nothing as they walked out to the parking lot together past the names of the dead on a sign encased in glass outside the church. SATURDAY EVENING MASS FOR BUBBA, it said in small block letters. No photographers or journalists permitted.

Josh walked with her to her car. She lit a cigarette and offered him one. He took it gratefully as they leaned against the car smoking and looking at the bright yellow marquee at the end of the parking lot. Chloe hadn't noticed it on her way inside. Looking at it now, she realized how strange it was that she hadn't seen the sign, even as she'd passed it turning into the parking lot. LORD SAVE BUBBA, it said across the top. And then, on the bottom in much smaller letters, BINGO WEDNESDAYS 6 P.M. Cash prizes.

Josh blew out a cloud of smoke and gestured toward the sign. "My mother took Darlene and me to bingo when we were kids," he said, flicking his cigarette at the grass beside the car. "You ever play?"

Chloe dropped her cigarette and ground it under her heel.

"When I was a kid, yes," she said, taking out her car keys and moving toward the door. "But not in a long, long time."

Josh nodded, brought the box closer to his chest, and held it with both hands.

"Did you ever win?" he asked.

She imagined Josh and Darlene running through the church parking lot, their looks of concentration as they played bingo shoulder to shoulder, elbows touching as they reached into the jar of chips they always shared.

"Sometimes," she said. "I used to play with my brother. But I'm afraid bingo's not my game."

They stood leaning against the car and smoking for a long time before either of them spoke again. She didn't mind the silence, though she knew that Nathan would have written some powerful lines for this exchange, perhaps the best he'd ever imagined. For this reason, she wished he were there with her, but there was something oddly comforting about being with Josh, leaning against a car and smoking with someone else's brother.

"Did you know the father?" she asked suddenly, and as soon as she said the words, she was sorry, even covered her mouth in embarrassment.

His cigarette glowed in the cool afternoon sun. He didn't seem upset by the question, but took several well-calculated puffs and shook his head.

"It's weird," he said finally. "All these people asking me questions about my sister and making a big deal about freaks."

He tossed the cigarette butt into the parking lot. It spun around several times and landed under a rhododendron.

"You have a brother, you said, right?"

Chloe nodded.

"Do you really know him?"

She smiled and thought of all the times her mother had accused her
of that very thing. "You think you know your brother, but you don't,"
she always said. "There's a lot more to him than Spider-Man."

"No," she said evenly. "I don't know him at all."

She turned the key in the lock and stepped aside as Josh held the
door open for her. He smiled down at her as she slid into the driver's
seat, the scar above his eye more pronounced in the sun.

"I'm going away for a while after all this," he said, looking out across
the parking lot at the church, his eyes moving over the stone crucifix
that hung on the side of the building. "People just don't get me right
now. We're all a bunch of freaks."

Chloe wished him luck as she buckled her seatbelt. She rolled down
the window and took a long look at him.

"Thanks for the doll, Esther," he said, leaning down before closing
the car door. "I mean, Chloe. I'll give it to my sister. I promise I will."

She told him she believed him because she did, waved to him as she
pulled out of the parking lot, watching in her rearview mirror as he
stood with the box under his arm. As she drove, she thought of Darlene
alone in her bedroom at night with no one to really know her, of poor
Bubba alone in the world, and of the woman with the third leg that
protruded from her belly, the way she'd tattooed her name on it as a
means of remembering who she really was.

Nathan went back to party planning after a week, having committed himself to an upscale retirement party with a Broadway theme for which he had to pay royalties of several thousand dollars to some long-running shows. He'd worked all night on a script that was a cross between *Hello, Dolly* and *Bye-Bye, Birdie*. He'd read snatches of the script to Chloe, but many of his lines seemed to have lost their earlier pizzazz, the majority of them falling flat.

"Ah, what the hell," he said before kissing her good-bye. "Let them think of what to say."

Chloe kept the television off and took in the daily newspapers. Each morning she'd hurry out to the front stoop and pick up the paper, folding it quickly in half and only opening it once she was in her work room. Thousands had lined up to try to adopt Bubba, and adoption officials assembled a task force to handle the inquiries.

Mostly she sat in her work room smoking and looking at a close-up of Josh in his tattered denim jacket with a white box tucked under his arm, the words "Neighbors Claim Three-Legged Woman Visits Mulholland Home" beneath his photo. She dragged deeply on her cigarette and exhaled, watching the smoke wrap around the sides of Josh's tired face.

Her mother's voice filled the machine day after day with updates on Irv's condition, her voice hoarse with longing every time she pronounced his name.

"Ralph seems to be getting better every day," her mother said. "It's hard on my boy, though. It's hard on all of us."

Chloe sat and smoked her cigarettes quietly and listened to her mother's breath.

"Yes, it is," she said aloud. Then she erased each message her mother had left.

Gloria Rollins called one morning while Chloe was still in her bathrobe, the smell of cigarettes thick in her hair. It was time to enter a doll for an upcoming show on the Eastern tip of Long Island, Gloria said, and the competition was going to be fierce. The show was expected to receive attention from the press and would attract the most avid collectors in the country.

"This is the big time, kiddo," Gloria said. "Time to show them what you've got, you and that Esther Bing you're so fond of."

Chloe sat writing her name in magic marker on her drawing pad as Gloria rattled off her ideas for the show. They could begin with a mock bingo game, she said, with Chloe and Gloria dressed as Bingo Ladies.

"I'll carry a blotter as I throw my dolls around," Gloria said, "and you can smoke to your heart's content."

Though she appreciated Gloria's enthusiasm, Chloe said she would enter the competition, but she would not appear as a Bingo Lady.

Reporters said a doll bearing Bubba's likeness had been left at the Mulholland family home after Josh's departure, where it lay in a bassinet in Darlene's old bedroom. No one had been able to determine who had made it. The real Bubba had been placed with an anonymous foster family on Long Island, his picture gracing the covers of several magazines on the newsstands. His head no longer looked quite so large, as if his adoption into normal life had shrunk the oversized skull, easing the fluid that had been weighing on his brain.

On the day of her sentencing following a guilty plea to charges of abandonment, Darlene Mulholland appeared pale and waxy in front of the judge. None of her family had appeared with her, one reporter said, and some had suggested that Darlene had chosen to face the judge alone. Chloe dragged the television into her work room where she watched the former homecoming queen stand with her head down, her hair bristly at the sides where she'd shaved off her curls.

"I wanted to be queen," she told the judge in a tremulous voice. "May God forgive me."

Chloe blew a cloud of smoke at the screen and touched the sides of Darlene's face before snapping the television off.

After several weeks of pining over ideas—Bingo Ladies with call numbers tattooed on their forearms like Holocaust survivors—she'd finally decided on a three-legged self-portrait. The doll didn't look like Chloe, exactly, but instead looked the way Chloe imagined others saw her. The face was narrow, drawn at the jaw line, with deep searching eyes made of blue-green marbles. A thin cotton nightgown hung off the shoulders and pushed up to reveal a shocking white belly and a pair of loose-fitting panties with daisies embroidered at the seams. It had taken her a week to finish the third leg, which she attached with horsehair stitches and stuffed with blue nylon for the tendons and pulsing veins. In lilac thread she'd sewn the name, Chloe, in small script letters that appeared to be little more than a web of varicose veins. Only on close inspection could anyone see that the stitches spelled out a name.

She was finishing the last of the stitches when her mother called. With the needle still poised in one hand, the thread coming through the nylon flesh and out again, Chloe answered the phone rather than let the answering machine fill the room with the sound of her own voice.

"My boy is finally home," her mother said before Chloe even had a chance to say hello. "He seems to be himself again. Our prayers have been answered."

She knew her mother had lit several candles in church for Irv and that she'd called upon Father Merritt for counseling though he'd begged off on account of chest pains. Twice she'd had Irv's name spoken at Sunday Mass during prayers for the sick, a favor she said she had coming to her after all she'd been through.

"My boy is back," her mother choked through the receiver. "Father Merritt was right. If families can only learn to cleave, then anything is possible."

Chloe set the three-legged doll on the table and knotted the last stitch. She held the doll up to the light and turned her to the left and right, marveling at the way the leg hung so easily from the middle, not dragging the nylon away from the armature with its weight. She'd worried about stuffing the leg with too much polyfill for fear of marring its paradoxical beauty, a misplaced appendage so delicate and ladylike in its pale simplicity. Yet she wanted people to be struck by the incongruity of this protrusion on an otherwise perfect belly.

"Did you hear me, Chloe?" her mother asked, the sudden shrillness of her voice nearly causing Chloe to drop the doll on the floor among the pieces of torn remnants and tattered fibers. "Your brother is home."

Chloe traced her finger over the space where the leg was sewn tightly to the intricate nylon-covered body.

"Yes," she said, reaching over for a new pack of cigarettes and lighting one. "I heard."

"Oh," her mother said, as Chloe exhaled the smoke in her mouth, a long silence hanging in the air between them.

She said good-bye and placed the receiver on the cradle. She held the doll down with one hand on its chest and stood up from her chair. With her other hand she tugged at the third leg, ripping it free. The horsehair stitches popped, bits of polyfill poking from the hole where the doll's navel should have been. She cradled the leg in her palm and stared down at the doll's wound above the daisy-lined panties, the nylon rolling into itself as if trying to keep the insides of the doll from spilling out.

They did not attend Irv's homecoming party. Chloe couldn't bear the thought of all of them sitting in metal folding chairs, Irv with his eyes glazed and a newborn's screams replacing his own. Instead she and Nathan drove to the doll show where she was to display the new doll along with several of her Bingo Ladies. The Big E had invited them to a weightlifting match in the area the following week where he would be the guest judge. After five years in retirement, he was eager for a tournament, he said.

"I've cleaved long enough," he'd told Chloe that morning on the phone. "It's time to pump iron again."

He told her that he'd miss her at the party, but that he understood why she didn't want to attend after all that had happened. Her mother wasn't happy with the decision, he said, though now that she had Irv back, she'd get over it soon enough.

Ruth had sent several snapshots of baby Irv in his Onesies, his eyes closed with a red pacifier between his lips. She'd enclosed a note with the photographs on stationery lined with green and yellow teddy bears. Spider-Man was nowhere to be found.

Dear Aunt Chloe, the note had said. *Please don't forget us. Love, Little Irv.*

Chloe folded the note carefully into fourths and tucked it inside her purse for safekeeping. On the way to the show, Nathan drove more slowly than usual, keeping it to sixty-five and passing on the right only once.

The hall was filled with signs marking the dollmakers' booths. Her space had a large white sign with her name marked in purple letters: Esther Bing, it said, and beneath her name: Bingo Ladies.

Gloria found her at the booth, where she kissed Chloe's cheek and gave her a rag doll that hung uneasily from her muu-muu.

"Here you go," she said, winking at Nathan before turning to head back to her own booth. "For luck."

Chloe and Nathan worked for a long time as they set up her booth, lining up her dolls along the table. She placed the newest doll closest to the front, where Nathan carefully positioned her and ran a finger softly over the batting poking from her middle.

Nathan reached down behind the booth and unfolded an enormous bingo sign on yellow oaktag. *Win big at bingo,* he'd written, *cash prizes.* They pinned the sign to the front of Chloe's booth, Nathan writing numbers on the corners and along the bottom.

"I've written you some good lines about bingo," he said, "but you don't have to say them unless you want to."

She smiled at him, as they stood beside the dolls with their blotters at the ready, the latest doll with her nightgown shiny under the fluorescent lights, her skin smooth but for the space where the third leg had been.

Chloe smoothed the doll's hair and looked around the room at all of the dollmakers standing along the rows of long tables, waiting for the crush of collectors. She smiled at the judges as they filed in, stopping to inspect each doll, making notes on clipboards and nodding their heads. One of these many dollmakers would be the lucky winner. With so much talent in one room, she knew the chances of winning first prize would be slim. Still, for tonight, if only for this one night, Chloe hoped that when the judges announced the prizes, that hers would be the voice to fill the room with triumph, the pure exhilarating scream of having won.

EPILOGUE

On Monday afternoons they play bingo. She loves Mondays for this reason, not because she loves the game and not because she ever wins—they are, of course, not allowed to win real prizes—but because bingo on Mondays helps her to get through the week. Bingo gives her something to look forward to, a change of routine, away from laundry or cafeteria duty. On Sunday nights she wonders if her luck is changing, if the parole board will hear her plea, if she will ever see the baby again.

Not that she has seen the baby since the day she was sentenced when the judge showed her a photograph of Bubba swaddled in pastel blankets and said in her ear, so close that she could feel the judge's breath, "Look at what you threw away."

Nights in prison are long; she is not surprised by this, though her lack of surprise does not make living through them any easier. At night she lies alone in the dark and imagines the baby fighting to kick the blue teddy bears that hang from a mobile above his crib. Sometimes she hears him crying and wakes with sweat pooled between her breasts, calling, "Mama! Mama!" until one of the other women screams at her to shut up and she realizes that she is the one who is crying.

She loves Sunday nights, too, because on Sundays they receive Communion. Someone called a Eucharistic Minister, a woman who looks a lot like her mother, actually, with her blue barrette and graying hair, teaches her the word "Eucharistic." She likes the way the word feels on her tongue, and, though she isn't Catholic, she says the word alone in the bathroom stall or while she folds the endless amount of clean, white towels in the prison laundry.

"The Body of Christ," the woman says, and she watches as the lines of women cup their hands and slide the circular wafer over their tongues.

Once she waited for one of the older women and asked her how the wafer tasted.

"Like shit," the woman said, "But everything that's good for you tastes that way, doesn't it?"

She supposed that was true, but still, she hoped it wasn't, not where the wafer was concerned.

In the beginning people from all over the country wrote letters, but now she gets mail only from three people. Her mother writes in black ink once a week and tells her about her days, what she and her father ate for dinner, whether they ate dessert or decided to take a walk instead. Her mother never mentions the baby, though Darlene wishes she would.

Josh is working on her appeal and writes when he stops long enough in a certain town to have something to say. He's found her a new lawyer, he tells her in a careful print she cannot recall him ever having, one who will have the "freak defense" reinstated if necessary. The woman he travels with is "different," he says, and Darlene doesn't ask him what this means.

"I may not have been the best brother," he writes. She thinks of telling him about playing bingo and how she wonders how the Eucharist tastes, but she does not answer his letters.

She keeps her letters hidden under her mattress, even though she is allowed to have them, where she can feel at the slips of paper at night, the bits of other people's rage on her behalf because that is the only rage she feels.

Her favorite letters come from a woman named Chloe. One day, after a bingo game, the officer in charge sent for Darlene to deliver a Fed Ex package. She'd thought it was her crown, the one her mother had saved for her, having glued the rhinestones back in place and reset on a gold wire. When she didn't recognize the return address, the officer said she couldn't allow her to open the package.

"But it's mine!" she'd said, weeping for the first time since any of it had happened, the pregnancy, the trial, the loss of Bubba. "It's mine, can't you see? Why can't I just have what's mine?"

Apparently the guard had taken pity on her because she'd since found out that none of the other women or girls her own age had ever been permitted to receive a package delivered not during regular mail hours. When she'd opened the package and found the doll inside, the baby she'd walked over in the locker room stall dressed in a white towel and smelling of nylon skin, she suddenly felt the knots in her stomach loosen, the terrible tightness that had wrung through every part of her finally start to give way.

"Dear Darlene," the letter began, "you don't know me, but I am a dollmaker. I used to be called Esther Bing, but you can call me Chloe."

A new letter arrives every Monday with Chloe's name stamped on the back. She has retired the Bingo Ladies, she writes, because she is interested in making other kinds of dolls now, though she is careful not to discourage Darlene from playing the game. Something terrible happened to Chloe a long time ago, Darlene knows, though Chloe has never told her what it was that happened, or what made it quite so terrible. But she knows that, for Chloe, the world at night is still not quite safe, and this Darlene understands.

In her letters to Chloe, Darlene feels herself becoming larger. She writes long sentences that curve over the margins and snake back in again, pages and pages of ink that stain her fingers and make her wrists cramp. She asks about Chloe's husband and how she knows she loves him, how she is able to fit him inside the space where the terrible thing happened. Chloe says she doesn't know how to explain except to say that she's gotten lucky, perhaps, in that she's learned to have a little faith.

Most nights Darlene cannot sleep. She keeps the Bubba doll in the bed beside her. Together they huddle under the blanket. In the darkness, to keep from being afraid, she tries to think of what she might write next, and what Chloe will say in reply.

She misses the baby. She misses him so much that her throat and chest begin to ache, and she holds the doll until she can breathe again, until the pain subsides, though she knows it will never fully go away.

Good books are brewing at coffeehousepress.org